5-85
16-
3-
Fran

‖‖‖‖‖‖‖‖‖‖‖‖‖‖‖‖‖‖‖‖‖
◁ **W9-DEW-319**

The two surgeons worked with efficient speed, in a delicate race against time. They had almost a dozen stitches in place when they both noticed a sudden change in the heartbeat.

"The heart's in block," Adam said soberly.

The chill of apprehension that telegraphed through the room could almost be felt. Heart block could happen with even the most meticulous surgeon, especially when he was stitching into the interventricular wall.

"Cut the needles and take out that last stitch," said Adam, "and let's hope."

The sudden sound of the sliding doors, opening with an abrasive force never before known in OR-4, startled the tense operating team.

It was Dr. Victor Strang. "Stop that operation!" he shouted. "It wasn't authorized by me!"

OPERATING ROOM - 4

by

ROY SPARKIA

PYRAMID BOOKS • **NEW YORK**

All of the characters in this book are ficticious, and any resemblance to actual persons, living or dead, is purely coincidental.

OPERATING ROOM—4

A PYRAMID BOOK

Copyright © 1973 by Roy Sparkia. All rights reserved. No part of this book may be reproduced or transmitted in any form or by any means, including photocopying, recording or by any information storage and retrieval system, without permission in writing from the Publisher, except for brief quotes used by reviewers for publication in a newspaper or magazine.

Printed in the United States of America

First edition, November 1973

ISBN 0-515-03078-3

Library of Congress Catalog Card Number: 73-85656

Pyramid Books are published by Pyramid Communications, Inc. Its trademarks, consisting of the word "Pyramid" and the portrayal of a pyramid, are registered in the United States Patent Office.

Pyramid Communications, Inc., 919 Third Avenue, New York, N.Y. 10022

CONDITIONS OF SALE

"Any sale, lease, transfer or circulation of this book by way of trade or in quantities of more than one copy, without the original cover bound thereon, will be construed by the Publisher as evidence that the parties to such transaction have illegal possession of the book, and will subject them to claim by the Publisher and prosecution under law."

OPERATING ROOM-4

PROLOGUE

He was about an hour out of Detroit, driving at a steady 65, when he felt the familiar pang under his breastbone.

"Goddammit . . ." he said softly and automatically reached for the packet of amyl nitrite capsules, at the same time remembering, because he had traveled this road so often, that the big Tri-County General Hospital was only fifteen or twenty miles ahead. Maybe he should stop for a quick check. On the other hand, he hated to waste the time if it wasn't absolutely necessary. These chest pains had been coming and going once or twice a week now for the past six months and not getting any worse.

With a heavy thumb he expertly crushed the little glass capsule into a handkerchief, held it against his nose and breathed in the stinging fumes. That should fix him up.

But it didn't. The pain was increasing as if from the relentless jaws of a vise inside screwing tighter.

Checking the rear vision mirror, he waited for a break in the fevering line of afternoon factory traffic in the next lane and skillfully eased the big Cadillac over to the far right of the wide freeway. He didn't want to miss the hospital exit.

Last time it felt this bad, couple years ago, the pain lasted all day. He was taking nitroglycerine tablets then but they didn't help. Everyone said he looked like hell. Finally one of the boys rushed him to a hospital where they slapped him right into ICU and he had the attack there.

Couldn't say they didn't warn him. Cut down the travel, the cigarettes. He was still smoking three, four packs a day, but he'd quit for sure, soon as he got out of the stinking ratrace. Maybe next week. After this trip, the organization could go to shit for all he cared. He could retire to Florida and never have another thing to worry about as long as he lived.

Christ . . . those pains! Like a goddamn elephant on his chest. Sweat slimed his face. Hastily he crushed another amyl nitrite capsule into the handkerchief and pressed it to his nose . . .

By the time he reached the hospital exit, there was a vague roaring in his ears. He had difficulty making the turn because a numbness was creeping into his shoulders and arms. He drove up a curving road to the main entrance of the hospital, stopped, and threw open the car door with his right hand because the left was almost useless now.

Getting out, he suddenly remembered the bag hidden under the back seat. Damn—he couldn't leave that behind!

The bag seemed to weigh a ton. He staggered forward with it for a few steps. *For God's sake*, he screamed silently at the towering walls, *why doesn't somebody come out and help me?*

Then came a great blackness, a giant hand pressing down, and Karl Lentz collapsed on the hospital front lawn . . .

one

. . . the scalpel sliced and all at once the heart was bared for all to see, an awesome thing of beauty, almost golden with blendings of lavender and plum and striations of venous blue, a fist-sized object that had begun to pulse and beat when no larger than a kernel of wheat in a mother's womb. And now it was dying. Fluid returning from the lungs no longer carried the oxygen of life. The pumping was frenzied, begging for relief that would not come, fibrillating in confusion and fatigue, the beautiful rhythm broken and translated to the EKG screen as an erratic green line of ventricular peaks and wild jerks but still struggling to flutter upward like a dying bird, only to fall again and again to the flat horizon of death.

Suddenly it turned threatening—a bloated thing rolling and heaving like an angry sea, dark with the storms and sins of a lifetime, a monstrous object thrashing crazily in the final isoclectric phase, but refusing to die . . .

He could stand it no longer, and cut again. The ugliness burst, engulfing him in waves of blackness . . .

Awakening from the nightmare he was at first dully surprised to see that bright morning had arrived, then puzzled by the strangeness of the room, and finally—when he rolled around to see who had awakened him—astonished. She had sea-green eyes and cornsilk blonde hair that shimmered all the way down to her naked breasts, and offhand he didn't know who the hell she was.

"What is it, Doctor?" she said. "Bad dream?"

It had to be, he thought, some kind of immunosuppressive antigen that builds up in their systems after years of exposure to enemas, bedpans, peevish patients and arrogant doctors. The best nurses, whether in soothing a dying geriatric case suffering intense pain or merely chiding a child for refusing the oatmeal, all had that same calm, firm cheeriness of voice. His less-than-instant recognition of her was because during the several years he had known her—on a purely professional level—he had never before seen Ilse Jensen, R.N. without the big round lavender-tinted glasses she habitually wore in the hospital, and with her hair down. Usually the pale gold tresses were gathered tightly in an austere upsweep, sometimes braided, and nearly always mostly hidden under a regular nurse's cap or an OR scrub cap.

"Horrible," he said, "but the awakening is truly beautiful."

She smiled. "I'm so glad. It's a shame you can't say the same about going to bed last night—or don't you remember?"

Dr. Adam Cane, Surgical Fellow and assistant to the Director of Surgery at Tri-County General Hospital, frowned and ran fingers through his disarrayed shock of black hair. "I have to admit my memory is still pretty damn foggy . . ."

"That's because you were pretty damn stoned, Doctor. I had quite a problem getting you upstairs and undressed and into bed."

Adam propped himself to a sitting position against the headboard and let his glance drop to the little curlings of hair across his broad chest and down between the ribcage of his flat torso. He grinned wryly.

"You're very capable."

"Unfortunately, the best capabilities are very limited when dealing with a patient who is so completely *incapable* . . ."

"I was that bad?"

"Not bad. Hopeless."

He laughed. "My apologies. But still, a good nurse shouldn't have let me get so stoned in the first place."

"You didn't warn me soon enough that you only had a few gulps of coffee for lunch, and skipped dinner before the operation."

Adam closed his eyes and groaned. The *operation* . . . now it was all flooding back. No amount of drunkenness, or even the propinquity of lovely naked female flesh—which had already fired his blood with a beginning surge of physiological arousal—could for long suppress conscience and memory.

Surgeons, he thought, should before each operation take a shot of their own Scopolamine—a drug given to patients as a relaxant which also produces retroactive amnesia so that the traumatic few hours following the operation are completely wiped from memory.

Karl Lentz had been an unusual case. He had arrived at the hospital alone three days ago—to collapse on the front lawn. Rushed into ICU and brought back under the respirator, he had complained of intense thoracic pain, later diagnosed as acute coronary insufficiency. His heart simply wasn't getting enough oxygenated blood. Arteriograms showed the overworked left ventricle swollen out like a bag. The coronary vessels were so clogged that the flow of blood to the heart was only a fraction of what it should be, and in one portion of the heart—revealed by X-rays to be ischemic from a past heart attack—there was no flow at all. It was a miracle that he was still alive, and at this point the massive damage to the heart and other vital organs was so far advanced that the patient could never again expect to get out of bed and go through a normal day without virtually certain death.

The only hope for Lentz, as spelled out by Dr. Victor Strang, hospital Director of Surgery and a famed cardiovascular surgeon, was a coronary artery bypass—a delicate high-risk operation in which a vein borrowed from the patient's leg is hooked up within the heart to give it a better supply of blood. And the sooner the better. To which Lentz had eagerly assented.

The operation had been performed last night . . .

"Do me a favor, Ilse. Put a call through to the Recovery Room . . ."

"I already did . . . a couple hours ago while you were still snoring." She hesitated, face clouded—"Karl Lentz is dead."

She was propped against the headboard, half turned to face him. His eyes slid down the lovely symmetry of her torso to the fringe of golden pubic fuzz showing above the sheet that draped her knees and thighs. Desire had fled.

"We murdered him . . ." he said.

"Adam, let's not start *that* again."

"You saw what happened."

"I saw Vic Strang operate, yes. But since you only did the preliminary cutting, and since you had nothing whatever to do with the bypass surgery involved, why don't you just forget it and stop acting like an intern who's lost his first D. O. A.?"

"How can I forget a blunder that cost a life we should have been able to save?"

"You don't really *know* that Vic blundered."

"I *do* know—and I didn't do anything about it."

"From where I sit, Dr. Cane, you did far too much. You very unwisely opened your mouth and said things to the great Dr. Victor Strang that nobody but *nobody* ever says to him. I can assure you he's not the kind to ever forget."

Adam furrowed his brow worriedly. He had indeed committed one of the cardinal operating room sins— but not until after he had seen how badly things were going.

The first inkling of things wrong had been when Strang dropped a small pair of iridectomy scissors—a trivial matter in itself since Ilse, as the instrument nurse, instantly slapped a replacement pair into his hand—but for the nerveless, precision-fingered Strang to be guilty of such clumsiness was astonishing.

The next slip was far more serious. In clearing a bit of fatty tissue away from the graft site, the heart itself was inadvertently cut into. Although Strange at once sutured the error with silk and needle, precious minutes were lost. In open heart surgery, speed was all-important. Five minutes lost could make the difference between life and death. Karl Lentz' body had already been subjected to the massive assault of being sliced open from the neck to a point just above the navel, the tough breastbone sawed through, veins cut and cauterized, the whole rib cage spread apart with retractors. Three or four electrodes had been attached to his head to monitor brain waves and see if it was getting enough oxygenated blood. An array of other probes sprouted from various parts of his body to carry intravenous fluids and measure arterial pressure, venous pressure, temperature, urinary output, and other bodily function-ing. The entire blood supply had been shut off from the heart by aortic clamp and drained through tubing into the heart-lung pump to be oxygenated—normally the work of the lungs—and then pumped through other tub-ing back into the body. Many things could go wrong, and one of the dangers was that if a patient was kept too long on the pump, his blood lost the ability to clot and could become acidotic—an over-abundance of lac-tic acid quickly leading to death.

Watching Strang at work, Adam's fears had grown. He knew from assisting at hundreds of operations per-formed by the master that the surgical director's usual speed and deftness were lacking. Strang had lifted from a metal basin the section of vein that had been stripped from the patient's thigh and flushed in saline solution for use as a detour vessel graft. Unbelievably, the skilled fingers were wavering and the surgeon frowned at the dangling vein as if unsure of what to do next.

Tense with awareness of the relentless ticking of the operating room clock and believing that his superior must be ill or overtired, Adam made his first big tacti-cal mistake.

"Vic," he said carefully, "if you'd like—if you're not feeling up to par—I'd be glad to take over."

Strang whirled, the pale blue eyes above his mask ablaze. "Doctor—when or if I ever need you to take over for me, I'll be the one to let you know!"

Bending over the patient, Strang then began the most meticulous phase of the operation, the most delicate, gut-wrenching procedure known to surgery—the sew-ing of one end of the transplant vein into the aorta and the other into a coronary artery buried within the heart itself—roughly equivalent to stitching the end of a piece of limp spaghetti into a soft wall of liver. Per-fectly and without leakage. As one eminent heart surgeon put it, "You practice for this by circumcising gnats."

Despite the air-cooling, Adam felt a beading of perspiration under his mask as he watched the other surgeon's fingers plying the needle and 4-00 silk. Was it only his imagination or was Strang really working with such stiff slowness? Was the suture line really so uneven? At one point Adam could barely restrain calling out in warning when the needle seemed to go too deep, too close to that vital clump of nerves called the Bundle of His. A single suture straying one millimeter into this clump could destroy the heart's natural pacing system, and the patient—if he survived—would for the rest of his life have to be wired up to a pacemaker.

A half hour of silence passed—an eerie cacophonic silence composed of beeping monitors, the swishing rhythm of the heart-lung pump and the *caw, caw* sound of the sucker draining leakage from the pericardium. And human breathing . . .

Finally Strang straightened, glanced at the clock, then reached down and removed the aorta clamp. At once, blood began flowing through the new vascular plumbing into the undernourished, dying part of the heart. Triumph gleamed in his eyes as his glance sliced past Adam to the two resident surgeons who were part of the operating team.

"Get him off the pump," he ordered, "and close the chest."

As they moved into position to complete the final and relatively simple phase of the operation, Adam signaled them to wait.

"Vic," he said mildly, "don't you think that first we ought to check it over?" It was a basic surgical tenet that Strang himself had so often emphasized—that after stitching, the suture line had to be carefully inspected for any sign of abnormal bleeding or faultiness of sewing that might later blow under a rise in blood pressure.

Strang seemed to swell beneath his surgical greens as if about to explode, but when he spoke, the voice was controlled icy venom.

"Are you questioning the surgery, Doctor?"

"I just think we ought to be goddamned sure, *Doctor*," Adam shot back, "because once the chest is closed, we can't go back."

Strang swung around to face the rest of the operating team, and now his words rose to a shout:

"Does anybody else here question my competence?"

There was, of course, no response. In the Operating Room, the ranking surgeon reigns supreme.

"I gave my order," snapped the surgical director. "Now hop to it and get him sewed up!" He strode out.

As the resident surgeons and others of the team moved into place to finish the job, Ilse Jensen came over to Adam.

"Doctor Cane," she said softly, close to his ear, "I think you could use a stiff drink—and so could I . . ."

Not until much later—while drinking his second double martini in a darkened little bar about a mile from the hospital—did Adam remember his tentative date with Glenna Woods. He had told Glenna, who was Strang's secretary, that he would call her after the operation and they could then decide on a place to meet for a late supper together.

But it was already too late, he rationalized, and he was still too angered and upset to make good company. To telephone and try to explain—with his voice already beginning to slur from the vicious assault of martinis on an empty stomach—would only worsen matters. He would apologize to Glenna tomorrow.

There *had* been gaps in the suturing, he kept telling

himself. He had *seen* them. He had also seen that clumsy slip, that inadvertent cut into the heart, and strongly suspected that at least one of the sutures had hit a nerve. That the brilliant Victor Strang—long noted for the clean perfection of his surgery—could be guilty of such a sloppy performance was incredible, mystifying—but a fact. It couldn't be just an aberration of his imagination. Or could it?

By this time, Adam's brain was too alcohol-slurred to be sure of anything—too fuzzy even to puzzle about why the usually aloof Ilse Jensen was suddenly so friendly.

For it was well known among the male members of the medical staff that Ilse was not only Strang's prize scrub nurse, but also his jealously-guarded private playmate with whom he spent much more of his free time than he did with his own beautiful socialite wife at home . . .

He was thinking of that now as Ilse leaned close and kissed him on the lips. She had been right in saying that Strang was not the kind to forget. Or forgive. Adam's affront to his superior's towering surgeon's ego last night was bad enough—but how would Strang feel if stung in an even more vulnerable spot—a man's sexual ego—if he ever discovered that his mistress had spent the night in bed with his lowly assistant?

"Mmmmmmm . . ." she said, and then drew her lips away, frowning. "But darling, you're so unresponsive! It's an insult. You've simply got to forget about last night and start living in the present . . ." The silky touch of her fingers slid around his torso.

He thought, why not? At least he had the dismal satisfaction of knowing that any of the surgical errors made last night—if there really were any—would be exposed when they did a post on the body down in Pathology.

He bent toward her, again feeling aroused, and with a hard kiss crushed her back against the pillows.

Only moments later, in conformance with the immutable laws of perversity that control such situations, the phone started ringing.

"Maybe," she said in a perfume-musky whisper, "we can ignore it."

"You know better." It wouldn't be for him, of course, but the same rules that enslaved doctors to the electronic monster applied almost as inescapably to registered nurses.

Hastily draping a robe around her, she padded to the phone and answered. After listening for a few moments, she turned and extended the phone in his direction.

"For you, *Adam*." Her expression, he thought, was a malicious blending of Mona Lisa and a purring cat.

The caller was Glenna Woods.

"I'm sorry to disturb you, Doctor, but this is an emergency. I tried to get you at your apartment, then called Dr. Strang, who suggested I try to get you at this number." Her tone, predictably, was cold and flat as martini meltage.

"What's the emergency, Glenna?"

"The little girl, the VSD case, is going into heart failure. Dr. Wolff is with her now in ICU and would like you to come in as soon as possible."

"Tell Dr. Wolff I'll be there within the next half hour."

two

The interns and nurses referred to it (unofficially, of course) as the Death Ward because it was where the terminal cases were kept. Its location on the fourth floor of the Tri-County General Hospital was partly a matter of expedience—being directly beneath the Operating Rooms as well as adjacent to the Intensive Care Unit—and partly a reflection of the "patient-oriented" hospital policy that it was better, for psychotherapeutic reasons, to keep patients segregated in accordance with the spectrum of their dependency needs. In effect, this allowed a concentration of scarce specialists and equipment in the areas where they were most needed and also kept the less critical cases insulated from the depressive atmosphere of the doomed. Another practical reason was convenient access to the freight elevator known (also unofficially) as the "meat drop" by which bodies were lowered to the morgue in the basement for pick-up by cheerful morticians or, with the family's permission, to the porcelain-topped slabs to be split from breastbone to crotch like so many chickens in a butcher shop, and sometimes the skull sawed open too in a final check for the causal mechanisms of death.

The latest to embark on that final journey to the white-tiled, air-cooled chambers below was a patient who had ceased to be early that morning and was now just an object identified as Karl Lentz by a tag tied to a big toe. His shrouded body lay on a stretcher being rolled along on silent ball-bearing casters toward the freight elevator by an orderly, with Nurse Kerri Kozak helping.

Nurse Kozak's eyes were damp. It was an unprofessional weakness that even after a year at Tri-County (following her graduation from St. Mary's School of Nursing in Saginaw) she was still unable to control. Although she had known the patient for only the day before the operation—which had taken place last night—she had been touched by his sweet, fatherly demeanor, and because he was so all alone in the world. His only relative was a sister in a distant state who was too infirm to travel, and he had no close friends. His only visitor had been the black man, a Mr. William Wilson, who came late yesterday afternoon to pick up the bag that Lentz had brought with him to the hospital. Mr. Wilson, explained Lentz, was an employee and the bag contained valuable prototype equipment that had to be delivered to an associate company as soon as possible. He also confided that after a lifetime of hard work he had now accumulated all the financial security he would ever need, and more, and that as soon as he had sufficiently recuperated from the operation (never for a moment doubting that it would be successful) he had only one more important deal to conclude and then would be free to retire to Florida and really begin to enjoy life.

"How did you manage to lose this one, Kozak?" said the orderly, whose name was Mike Tunstra. He was about 28 and had a mop of stringy reddish hair askew over his ears and scraggly sideburns down to his jowls in imitation of a hard rock singer he admired.

"Heart failure."

"Heart, my ass." Tunstra spoke in the pseudo-cynical manner he had adopted in imitation of some of the residents and interns he despised and envied and, because of his hospital whites, fancied he looked like. "Let me set you straight, Kozak. Whenever *you're* involved, the problem is too much TLC. You hold on to them too long."

"In this case, not long enough, obviously."

"You don't grasp it, Kozak. This is the first stiff we've had in three days. Don't you realize that regular meat deliveries are our only job security down in Path? If all the nurses were as schmaltzy as you are, I could be out sitting on the curb."

"My prescription for you, Orderly Tunstra, is a brand new heart transplant!"

"In this charnel house? Then who'd roll me down to Path after old Dr. Jesus Strang, Super-Star, got through with me?"

"Don't worry. His last transplant lasted almost two years. That ought to be long enough for you."

"But how could I count on it? Look what he did to this trusting jerk. Who is he, by the way?" The orderly twisted his head around to look at the death card pinned to the top of the shroud.

"Karl Lentz," she said.

"You've got to be kidding!" Tunstra stopped the stretcher and carefully lifted a corner of the shroud to peer under. The dead face was relaxed and peaceful; the sagging wrinkles had the bloodless look of melting wax. "So *this* is old Lucky Lentz!"

"That's unkind," she said reproachfully, "to joke about him."

He stared at her. "You really don't know who this guy *is*? You never heard of Lucky Lentz? Didn't you read the morning papers?"

"No, I—"

"Haven't you even heard about that runner of his that was brought into EW last night all shot up?"

"I don't have time for gossip, and besides I've only been on duty for an hour."

"Christ, Kozak, if you can't read, at least tune in on the hospital vine and find out what's going on in the world. Old Lucky here is—*was*—a big numbers boss. He had hundreds of runners working for him in Detroit and all the big factories in the state."

Kerri knew, as did most people in lower Michigan, that the numbers game had spread from the Detroit ghettos into the factories to become one of the most popular games among blue collar workers. Although commonly known to be Mafia-controlled and the thousand-to-one odds almost impossible to beat, as well as mostly crooked, its appeal seemed to be irresistible to gambling instincts of the millions who didn't mind risking anywhere from a penny to a few dollars on the way, *way* out chance of windfall returns.

"You're putting me on," she said dubiously. "How do you know it's the same man."

"I just told you, for God's sake. That black boy who got shot up—probably by some Mafia creeps—was Speed Wilson—"

"Wilson?" That was the name of the employee she had telephoned, at Lentz' request, to come and pick up the bag late yesterday afternoon. "Was he also known as *William* Wilson?"

"How would I know?" Tunstra was suddenly disinterested. "Read about it for yourself, Kozak. Frankly, all this Mafia stuff is a big bore."

It couldn't really be true, Kerri thought defensively, remembering the kindly, respectable face of her recent patient. But if it was—then that bag could have been stuffed with money!

They reached the freight elevator, and she helped maneuver the stretcher inside but didn't enter herself. Nothing short of a direct order from a superior could have forced her down to the morgue, which she thought of as some kind of Hitchcock-inspired chamber of horrors. The indignity and outrage of a helpless, denuded corpse being chopped apart (invariably, she saw the gentle face of her mother in this context) was appalling. Even though she knew that autopsies were necessary to safeguard medical standards and increase medical knowledge, she was always secretly relieved when the family, for religious or personal reasons, refused consent.

"Why don't you come down and watch the Path chief cut him open?" said Tunstra, grinning because he knew her phobia about cadavers. "Maybe we'll find a pot of gold inside."

"Apparently you haven't noticed," she said with a special gleam of triumph in her electric blue eyes, "but this is one you're not going to touch." She tapped a slim finger against the death card, across which had been scrawled boldly, no autopsy, underlined twice.

Tunstra's mock groan muffled away behind the pneumatic wheeze of the closing elevator door.

One floor above in the small auditorium used for film and slide lectures, Dr. Hugo Barr, Director of Medicine and Medical Education, was in the midst of his little welcoming speech to the new batch of seventeen interns.

". . . as a reference point," he was saying, "let us hark back to the famed comment of the eminent L. J.

Henderson, who in 1910 said that the average patient visiting the average physician had only a fifty-fifty chance of benefiting from the encounter . . ."

A side door close to the podium opened and a gaunt-visaged nurse with stone-gray hair showing beneath her cap stepped inside.

"Dr. Barr, may I interrupt you for a moment?"

Barr frowned. "What is it, Rosemary?" He used the first name only because Rosemary Clugg was the Supervisor of Nurses and he had known her for many long years.

"There's a police officer downstairs who would like permission to station one of his men in Intensive Care near the patient who was brought in with bullet wounds last night."

Dr. Barr made it a point to keep informed about every patient entering Tri-County and remembered the case: a black male, about 28, shot while in a car only a couple miles from the hospital, and now in coma from multiple gunshot wounds, shock, and hemorrhage.

"For heavens sake, why?"

"In case he regains consciousness, they want to be on hand to question him as soon as possible, Doctor. The patient has a crime record and they believe he has vital information they need."

"You may tell the officer," Barr said testily, "that we have a vital concern in the patient's physical welfare, criminal or not, and under no circumstances will we allow police officers underfoot in ICU nor police interrogation of the patient until such time as it is deemed safe."

"Yes, Doctor," Nurse Clugg said dryly. "I'll tell him you said 'no'." She went out.

Dr. Barr glared, and then picked up his talk again at the exact point he'd left off, for it was almost verbatim the same speech he had delivered every July 1st—the traditional beginning day for new interns—for the past eight years.

". . . But that was over sixty years ago. Since then, the armamentarium of modern medicine has mushroomed fantastically. We now have enough diagnostic tools—for example, our myelograms, stereocinefluorographs, radioisotopes, ultrasound detectors, electroencephalographs, to name a few—to enable us to quickly and accurately pinpoint almost any physical ailment known to man."

Hugo Barr paused and let his bright little blueberry eyes, wryly encased in the sebaceous folds of a sedentary fifty-nine year old face, skim over the neophytes. Plainly they were bored. Their studied expressions of polite interest paid tribute only to their complete awareness that their careers and private lives, for the next year at least, would be almost entirely under his control. The ethnic and gender mix of this crop had broadened to include two women—one black and one white—and one black male. Diverse minority types running neck and neck, so to speak. Well, at Tri-County they'd learn soon enough they had to keep running. He wasn't dispensing any special favors.

"In other words, gentlemen—ah, and ladies—" the director smiled benignly and bowed his graying leonine head apologetically in the direction of the two women—"as fledgling physicians and as the true heirs and repositories of all the wisdom, art, and science of medicine that has accumulated during the twenty-three centuries since Hippocrates, you have powers beyond belief. Never before in all history have doctors been so knowledgeable—or his patients so fortunate. Does that not make you feel good?"

He saw they were more relaxed now, expressions pleased, responding to the call of American folklore— their lofty image as stethoscope-draped God-figures. And doubtless, for most of them, he had touched upon the primus of their motivations—Cadillacs and country clubs.

"Of course, this is not entirely bullshit," he added casually, noting with relish the delayed shock in a few faces who thought they had not heard correctly, "but it is my compelling duty to puncture the simplistic myth that American medicine today is characterized by a tremendous distribution of quality medical care. The euphemistic portrait of the modern super-doctor skillfully manipulating the entire arsenal of diagnostic and curative weaponry available to him—presumably to keep his patients healthier and living longer—is one of the most gigantic deceptions ever inflicted on millions of unsuspecting victims."

He paused for another breath then plunged on:

"The incredible truth—as amply proven by statistics, reports, surveys and studies pouring in daily—is that nationwide among today's patients, only forty percent of their ailments are found and labeled by the examining physician. Sixty percent are utterly missed! And of the forty percent ostensibly found, half are wrongly diagnosed. The appalling score is this: *today's average patient going to the average doctor with an unknown ailment has only one chance in five of having it diagnosed correctly.*"

The director's eyes, now grown hot with the intensity of his feelings, swept over the audience searching for guarded skepticism, the repressed grin. The first necessity was to penetrate their often arrogant, often thick little egos, to shake them up, open their eyes, stamp out the insidious beginnings of professional provincialism that could only add more shame to medical performance. The faces were discreetly expressionless.

"The surprise on your faces," said Hugo with heavy irony, "is understandable. And if perhaps you wonder why the record is so bad, it is simply because the vast majority of modern physicians are not using all the

medical knowledge, skills and tools at their disposal—
not necessarily from stupidity but simply because they
can't or won't take the time. Today's businessman-doc-
tor is too concerned with rushing patients through his
medical production line and piling up the dollars. In
short, he is skimping over the very cornerstone and
foundation of all medicine—diagnosis."

He paused again, this time not for effect but to take
a couple of deep breaths, for the director had a slight
emphysema problem.

"I repeat—" and now anger added harsh force to his
voice as he leaned forward, one clenched hand beating
against the open palm of the other for emphasis, "diagnosis, diagnosis, *diagnosis*! Without prompt and accurate diagnosis, all the rest of our wondrous medical
capabilities are worthless!"

He stood for a few moments in silence, aware of the
thickness in his chest—again he had over-expended his
breath. One of these days soon, he promised himself, he
would steal time from his duties to take the pulmonary
function tests.

"As you may have overheard a few minutes ago," he
went on tiredly, "we have in ICU a victim of criminal
brutality—a young man who may or may not die."

He turned and started off the podium platform.
"Now follow me and let us look in on some of the
cases who will most certainly die—the tragic victims of
doctor incompetence."

three

The morning, as can be predicted for any first day of July in the flat lower belly of the Michigan mitten, was hot and humid and laden with foreboding of turning into another scorcher. By afternoon, tempers would grow snappish, heart attacks soar among the elderly, production line absenteeism leap to new peaks, and all the beer gardens in the industrial heartland would be jammed to capacity with unquenchable guzzlers.

Dr. Adam Cane, driving fast on the wide freeway, bent to open the air vents. The whooshing indraft was redolent with gasoline fumes, a sulphurous tang of factory smoke, and a faint whiff of chlorophyll from the rows of baby corn in a nearby field and which—judging from the emaciated stalks—would never make it to the traditional farmers' standard of knee-high by the fourth of July.

Although the reason for his haste was eleven year old Holly Robbins going into heart failure from her ventricular septal defect, Adam's thoughts at the mo-

ment were less on the emergency medical problems
ahead than on his own long-festering personal problems
that had come to a head last night.

He could expect—and deserved—unhappy conse-
quences due to his stupid overdrinking, the hurt to
Glenna Woods, and the whopping blunder, unintended
as it was, of spending the night with the boss's girl
friend.

Yet these complications were trivial in comparison
with the major problem that increasingly bugged his
life.

Strang . . .

When he first came to Tri-County three years ago,
Adam had been elated at having swung a residency under the fabulous Dr. Victor Strang—one of the giants
in the rarefied world of heart surgery, right up there
alongside Barnard, DeBakey, Cooley, Kantrowitz,
Shumway, Lillehei—names to make any aspiring surgeon figuratively genuflect. At the time, Adam had just
completed two years of residency in huge Massachu-
setts General where he had felt somewhat lost in the
vastness, just one of the anonymous several hundred interns and residents. At the much smaller Tri-County
General Hospital, coming in as a senior resident directly under Strang, he felt sure that his opportunities
for gaining knowledge and operating experience in the
specialized field of his choice—thoracic and cardiovascular surgery—would be greatly enhanced.

He had been quickly disenchanted. Accustomed to
the academic, ordered medical program at Massachu-
setts, he found the chaotic but stern dictatorship of
Strang hard to adjust to. Strang ran the entire Surgical
Division as a one-man show, plainly intending to remain as the one and only star in the Operating Rooms.

After one year Adam advanced to Chief Resident,
after the second was honored by being made a Fellow
and assistant to Strang. The days of fixing hernias, tak-

ing out appendixes, removing hemorrhoids and other such simple procedures were long past. Now he scrubbed in with Strang on the big cases, an average of five or six operations a day. He did a lot of vessel work, opened chests for heart surgery and transplants, was even allowed to carry through the most delicate surgery under the master's close supervision. He knew he was damned good and rapidly getting better, and worked his guts out to prove it—which finally brought unexpected reactions.

Strang suddenly began to fault everything he did:

"What's wrong, Doctor? Did you think you were sewing up a pair of britches? Can't you even tie a simple knot? Now remove those stitches and see if you can't do it right!"

"For Christ sake, Doctor—don't you realize that under this drape we have a living patient—not a practice dummy? You've got to work faster!"

"The slant of your incision, Doctor—have you forgotten your anatomy? You're supposed to be headed for the kidneys, not slicing a Christmas turkey."

"It must be INTENTIONAL, Doctor—nobody could possibly do such a butcher job in getting the chest open unless he really WANTED to kill the patient!"

After harrowing weeks of this, Adam's confidence began to falter. It got so bad he was almost afraid to drape a patient for fear he wasn't doing it right. The chief anesthesiologist, Dr. Joe Oberholtzer, tipped him off:

"Don't let it throw you, Adam. Your only real trouble is you've revealed too high a degree of surgical talent."

"I don't get it, Joe."

"You've got to understand that Vic is basically paranoid. He's *got* to be number one. Close competition scares him. Just the thought of any of his subordinates catching up with him to share the glory—perhaps even getting a little ahead—drives him crazy."

"If that's the way he feels, then why the hell doesn't he kick me out?"

"Because he needs you, Adam. He couldn't carry on such a heavy surgical workload, and do it as well as he does, without the kind of help he gets from you. He knows this but at the same time doesn't want to admit it to himself. His ego compels him to minimize your talents, and he'll do all he can to hold you down to the level he wants you to stay on."

"What do you suggest I do?"

"Just play it cool. The big danger is he could start suspecting you of sneaking around behind his back to undercut him, or going over his head to the Board, or doing anything to jeopardize his supremacy—and it happens, too, because the suspicious paranoid, by his illogical, aggressive behavior screen thrown up to protect his own interests, actually *forces* talented underlings to adopt the very defense mechanisms the paranoid most fears. I suggest you swallow your pride, Adam. Take everything Vic wants to dish out and just keep a stiff tongue in your cheek."

"But there are limits!"

"The only limit as far as you're concerned is how far Vic wants to carry it. Keep in mind he's in a position to make or break you, so humor him for Chrissake. Crawl on your belly—anything that makes him feel better. You'll only have to suck hind tit for one more year of residency and then you've got it made. It's your big opportunity, Adam. Don't blow it."

The tactic seemed to work. Strang softened, perhaps sensing Adam's new imperturbability. Or perhaps it was that other thing . . .

The fact was that Strang was changing, accepting fewer of the geriatrics and the complicated cases, seeming to show less and less of his old technical brilliance and deft skills.

But Adam hadn't been sure of it until last night.

He braked and swung into the right lane. The hospital exit was just ahead, and about a quarter mile beyond, enclosed within an arterial loop of roads, sprawled the medical buildings beneath a haze of yellowish-gray smog.

For reasons best known to its founders, Tri-County General Hospital was located several miles from the suburban fringes of the nearest town on once-pleasant farmland now giving way to encroaching industry. Although still a smallish institution of about 350 beds, it was considered very progressive, well-staffed and well-equipped. The original old red brick general hospital had expanded into a rectangular complex of attractive new buildings including the Children's Pavilion on one side, the Clinic on the other, and in front—separated by an interior courtyard—the Administration building. The nurses' quarters were in a separate building and a wing had also been provided for the interns and residents who lived on the premises.

Turning, Adam saw police cars ahead, three of them lined up along the opposite side of the road. One with a revolving red beacon flashing on the roof.

He drove on slowly. An officer waved him on, at the same time holding up his other arm to stop a car coming from the hospital direction. What was up?

Shrugging inwardly, he picked up speed. He had no time for idle curiosity about a police blockade. The only question of any importance now was the life or death matter of Holly Robbins.

Nurse Kerri Kozak, returning from the freight elevator, was making an extra effort to maintain the usual cheery smile with which she strove to face patients, but it was hard. Encounters with death left her feeling emotionally drained and haunted for hours. She was still not inured to the atmosphere of morbidity and hopeless gloom, and doubted that she ever would be.

Among other things, she didn't like the smells. A pert and pretty girl with loam brown hair, vibrant cobalt eyes, and the exotic high-cheeked facial structure of her Bohemian ancestry, Kerri Kozak had grown up on a farm in lower Michigan sugar beet country accustomed to pollen-scented breezes and a family fetish of cleanliness not even outdone by the Dutch colonies several counties away where the women still went through the yearly rituals of hand-scrubbing all the paved streets in town. She equated health and happiness with nice smells, and conversely, the most horrid smells she had ever known were those she had to endure daily among the stricken and dying. For here, despite strict cleansing routines and constant air-conditioning, the miasma of sickness and decay, mingling with but unmollified by astringent medical odors, hung in the air—and indeed clung to clothing and furnishings—like a penetrating viral taint. Sour vomit, bedpans, the stench of incontinent defecations from various gastrointestinal disorders, the fungating, foul-smelling, sloughing exudates of inoperable cancer—the pitiable effluvia of the doomed.

In one bed lay a man straining against pillows propped behind him because his lungs were so sodden with edema that lying flat he would drown in his own juices. Fluids bubbled from his lips with each choking breath, making eerie high-sucking sounds in his frenzied efforts to get more air.

In another cubicle was a woman in her fifties who looked wizened and shrunken enough to be a hundred. The cancer spreading through her system had imparted a yellow, waxen translucence to her skin—and also driven her into periodic screaming agonies that even

Demerol could no longer alleviate. At times she passed to a threshold beyond pain where for awhile her face relaxed into a smile while her withered fingers played inaudible melodies on an invisible piano—the only part of her cancer-rotted brain still intact being that containing memories of happy childhood. Minutes later she would be screaming again.

Elsewhere a desperately ill old man with disseminated colonic cancer, recently transferred from a nursing home to die here, lay curled on his side in the fetal position making the whimpering, plaintive sounds of a puppy drowning in a well.

And dozens more: an unending influx of those who still breathed but for whom nothing more could be done. The tragedy for most of them, thought Kerri, was not that they would die soon—only that they weren't already dead.

Reaching the private room 403—so briefly occupied by Lentz before his operation last night—she saw that the next occupant was just being rolled in on a wheelchair and automatically wondered what it would be this time—coronary, cancer, aneurysm, gall bladder, pneumonia?

Then seeing the tall young man in summer slacks and jacket walking just behind the orderly, she knew. Natalie Tyler. Carcinoma of the breasts metastasized to the bones. And she was only twenty-six!

The shock of recognition must have shown on her face, for Dave Tyler, Natalie's husband, looked at Kerri with a strained smile.

"Yes, we're back again, Miss Kozak." His eyes had a misted redness.

"I—I'm really sorry," said Miss Kozak. What else could one say? They had known she was terminal when Natalie was brought in about ten months ago, when Kerri had first met her. One of Natalie's legs had given way that day on the golf course—the first inkling that the fulminating malignancy for which she had undergone radical mastectomy two years previously had not been fully eradicated after all, as the surgeons had "hoped", but had swiftly invaded the musculoskeletal system. Beyond surgical help, she was immediately given radioactive phosphorous treatments, but everyone knew that all that could possibly be done for her would only be a delaying action at best.

Everyone, that is, but Natalie. She radiated with supreme confidence that by sheer grit and will she could and would win out against the disease that had felled her. She had reason to think this way. She was still young, vital, very beautiful, and had always been one of the lucky ones. From an upperclass background, Radcliffe educated, married to a handsome young space engineer, a PhD, who did lucrative secret defense work for the missile program. She lived in a fine suburban home, had her own imported sportscar, an elaborate wardrobe, a maid—the whole world at her feet.

But when less than three months ago she had been brought in again for removal of ovaries and the adrenals in a last ditch effort to slow the destruction, her spirited optimism was gone, replaced by forlorn bravado. She had aged twenty years.

And now . . .

"Hello, Kerri—" The deep masculine pitch of Natalie's voice—a result of the heavy male hormone therapy she had been receiving—was another shock. "I hope you'll forgive me for not shaving, but Dave dragged me away in kind of a hurry."

Smiling to hide the revulsion she could not help feeling at the stubble of beard—another result of the male hormones—on the grayed, wrinkled face that only a few months ago had been so fresh and smooth, Kerri said brightly, "Don't fuss about it, Mrs. Tyler. We're well equipped here to handle little details like that."

"We specifically asked that you be assigned to Natalie," said Dave Tyler. "You were so good to her last time."

Natalie let out a croak of laughter.

"What other nurse would have the sublime beauty of soul to let Dave sneak in a thermos of cold martinis for me now and then? And remember the champagne on my twenty-sixth birth——?" She suddenly doubled forward, arms hugging her belly and shoulders jerking in accompaniment to stabbing spasms of pain. Agonized little sounds swiftly spiraled into nerve-clenching shrieks.

"Oh God——" she screamed. "I can't take it any more! Kill me, somebody—please, *please,* PLEASE!"

Kerri hurried forward. "Let's get her into bed," she said to the orderly.

"Stay away—stay *away* from me!" shrieked Natalie and began flailing an arm in the air to fend off Kerri's approach.

The floor supervising nurse, Loma Palmer, appeared. "I'll handle this, Miss Kozak." And to Natalie, "It's all right, dear. A doctor will be here in a moment. You're going to be fine, just *fine.*"

". . . there's nothing, but *nothing,*" Dave Tyler was saying in a misery-rooted voice, "that can help anymore . . . except maybe what she wants."

Another nurse, Miss Frohm, came up and tapped Kerri on the arm. "Miss Clugg wants you to report in her office right away, Kerri." Then she leaned close and whispered in her ear, "for *police* questioning."

Kerri hastened away, for the moment relieved to escape a situation where she felt so futile. Vividly imprinted on her mental screen was a last glimpse of the one who could not escape—the suffering husband. He had remained standing outside the room with head bowed and arms straight against his sides, fists clenched, as if in furious prayer. The piercing screams were subsiding.

Halfway down the corridor, she had to slow down to allow passage of a sizable group in hospital whites who were meandering along close behind Dr. Hugo Barr, the benign Director of Medicine and Medical Education. Realizing that they were the new batch of incoming interns, she made her face a cool, impersonal mask. She'd had enough encounters with young interns during the past year to know that there were always some of them quick to interpret her usual warm smile as an invitation for a little furtive necking in any deserted corridor, wardrobe closet, or room that happened to be empty, as well as implied willingness to visit their bachelor quarters, like that same night. Several of the older staff doctors had also propositioned her, sometimes not too subtly, and even a couple of the other nurses had made passes—perhaps assuming that her firm rebuffs to amorous males indicated that she was a potential lesbian (which Kerri definitely was not).

Actually, it was nothing new. Since high school days, Kerri had become aware that she possessed a certain quality—quite apart from her shapely figure and attractive face—that she neither understood nor wanted, something that convinced many males (mistakenly) that she was so bursting with sexiness that they just couldn't seem to keep their eyes and hands off. The truth was, Kerri didn't know how to cope with it—except by instant backing off into her cool, rigid shell of old-fashioned morality standards.

Ignoring the appraising glances, the well-meant smiles of appreciation from several of the passing interns, Kerri hurried on, her thoughts determinedly on the confrontation ahead.

The police? Why in the world did they want to question her?

Followed by his retinue of interns, Dr. Barr entered ICU which at the moment contained about a dozen beds, most of them filled with postoperative major surgery cases. The ghastly orange that had been painted on their chests and bellies and was still visible beneath swathings of bandages and tape, and from various parts of their anatomy sprouted a twisting conglomeration of wires and tubes and needles to monitor organ functioning, feed them intravenously, drain them intra-abdominally, and through which inched blood and urine. Imprisoned beneath all these spidery attachments to their flesh and also entrapped in pain and fear, some of them became psychotic. Having awakened in a strange windowless room with no hint of night or day—only eternal cold fluorescence more suggestive of hell than heaven—they were often disoriented, particularly the older ones, and sometimes struggled frantically to climb out of bed and rip away the life-preserving tubes and wires. At times it seemed they were battling against life, wishing to reject consciousness and return to the peace of nothingness.

Continuing on to a section of the room that had been curtained off, the medical director pushed through an opening between the drapes. One by one, the interns filed through after him.

Dr. Melton Kloster, the resident neurologist, who was bent over a young male patient with an ophthalmoscope studying the pupils of his eyes, looked up as the director entered.

"Any change, Mel?" said Barr.

"About the same as it's been since six-thirty this morning," said Kloster. "The pupils are still blown up, still dilated." He looked unhappily at the interns who were now crowding into the confined space, some of them casting curious glances at the Bird ventilator which was clicking on and off with its muffled *whoosh, whoosh* of air and oxygen pumping into the patient's lungs. His chest rose and fell every three seconds, about the same as it would have if the machine were not doing the work for him.

"How are the electroencephalogram readings?"

The neurosurgeon could have answered with only a word or two but he knew and approved of the hard-working medical director's reason for being here, even though it was an annoyance. These young people were here to learn, and a demonstration was always more effective than words.

"See for yourself," he said, and placed the electrodes of the electroencephalograph on the patient's skull. At once the stylus of the EEG apparatus nearby began to move across the graph paper—drawing a straight line. The interns watched, fascinated.

"The brain," Kloster went on, "registers no electrical activity whatsoever. No peripheral reflexes. No reaction to pain stimuli. The pineal has calcified and shifted."

"Would you please give our young doctors a history on this case, Mel?" said Barr.

Grudgingly, Kloster removed the electrodes, his admiration for Barr overcoming his dislike of lecturing. He knew that in private practice Barr could easily make over $100,000 to $150,000 in *admitted* income, but instead had dedicated himself totally to upgrading medical excellence with no thought of monetary rewards.

"If you'll notice," said the neurosurgeon, "this lad has an intercranial injury. The physician who first treated him had to shave away a lot of that beautiful blonde hair—I understand the patient complained bitterly at the time. That was last night following a little accident. The patient, who was driving a motorbike, ran it into a telephone pole and was thrown to the road where his head scraped against the curb, laying open a two-inch flap of scalp. It knocked him silly for a few minutes, but he wasn't unconscious. A friend rushed him to a doctor who cleaned up the mess—a lot of dirt and pebble grit embedded in the scalp—then sewed him up, gave him a few pills, and sent him home with orders to rest up in bed and come back tomorrow for a checkup. The bio-chemical lab, by the way, found evidence that at the time of the accident he had been hopped up on cannabis—that's pot, as I'm sure you doctors know." Kloster grinned wryly.

"The patient's concerned mommy," he went on, "tucked him into bed and was at first quite pleased that he fell asleep so nicely. Several times during the night she checked him and found him still apparently in peaceful sleep. Toward morning she began to get worried by the fact that he hadn't moved his position for several hours. She tried to awaken him, and got frantic when she couldn't—he was in a coma from brain hemorrhage. She then had the belated good sense to call an ambulance. We got him at about five this morning and had him in OR-3 twenty minutes later, but it was too late. Skull X-rays confirmed that the problem was extradural hemorrhage—blood collected between the skull and the meninges due to rupture of several branches of the middle meningeal artery—resulting in the severe compression of blood and swollen brain tissues that had already destroyed the brain."

After a pause, Dr. Barr said, "In your opinion, Doctor, what was the margin of time following the lad's accident last night when an operation might have saved his brain?"

"If, following the preliminary cleansing of the wound and sewing up the scalp, he'd been rushed up here, we could have diagnosed the problem and cut into the skull in time to prevent the hematomata—the accumulation of blood clots inside the skull—and stopped the bleeding."

"Then it was a preventable case?"

Kloster frowned. God knows he had committed his share of medical blunders—as had every other doctor he knew—but he didn't like putting the onus on any individual practitioner. Yet he knew it was useless to try to evade old Barr's bulldog insistence on pinning down responsibility.

"Unfortunately for the patient," he said, "his friend didn't have the foresight to bring him directly to a hospital emergency ward, much less a neurosurgeon."

"More to the point," Barr added tartly, "the doctor he took him to didn't have enough sense to know when he was in over his head. He should have insisted on skull X-rays before sending the lad home—an inexcusable diagnostic mistake."

Kloster said nothing. He, at least, was in the clear.

"As has been shown," the medical director went on grimly, "the brain is now dead, and nothing in this world can ever revive it. He has even lost the power to breathe. Only the machine breathing for him is keeping the body alive. In other words, he's medically dead." His glance skimmed over the somber faces of the interns. "Any questions?"

"Are you planning to use him as a transplant donor?"

Barr looked carefully at the speaker because he wanted soon to be able to identify them all by name and appearance, to begin evaluating their capabilities. The intern was tall, heavy-boned, with a rather wide face, palest blue eyes and almost white-blonde hair—the straight and intractable kind that stuck up in tufts here and there despite obvious efforts to comb it flat. Probably of Polish extraction.

"Your name, sir?" he asked.

"Steve Wolosyk."

"In answer to your question, Wolosyk, the patient would indeed make an ideal transplant donor. His healthy young kidneys, for example, could almost surely save another life, the cornea transplants might well restore the gift of sight to still another, and so on—but unfortunately, his family disapproves. The mother—quite understandably a bit hysterical—refuses to allow any smallest part of her son to be removed for the preservation or benefit of other lives, and of course we must abide by her wishes."

"Then what's the point of prolonging the vegetable existence of a brain-dead body?"

The director looked more sharply at Wolosyk—not because of the question but because of the quiet intensity with which it was spoken. Barr's own concept of the Slavic temperament was that it tended to be half poet, half pragmatist; stoic on the outside and highly emotional inside. The bony, flat-planed face was taut with repressed feelings.

"Do any of the rest of you gentlemen—uh, or ladies—aside from legal, ethical, or religious considerations, which aren't in question at the moment—see any good reason for keeping the body alive?

Except for a few negative murmurings, the interns were silent.

"In that case, Wolosyk," said Barr, "your opinion is borne up by everybody present, so please step forward and turn off the respirator."

Wolosyk, his face abnormally pale, stood rigidly unmoving.

"Go ahead, Wolosyk. Certainly you should be able to follow through on your convictions. The switch is plainly discernable on the right side of the respirator."

With jerky movements, Wolosyk strode forward and flicked off the switch. At once, silence draped over the room and the patient ceased breathing.

"Now ladies and gentlemen," the director droned on, "you have each become a party, by concensus, to doing a little of God's own dirty work for Him. In about fifteen minutes the patient will be entirely dead."

A heavy *ka-lumping* sound broke the silence, and looking to the cause, Barr saw that Wolosyk had collapsed to the floor. Before he could issue an order, the black girl was already kneeling beside the fallen intern.

"Everyone please step back," she said in a soft, calm voice, "and somebody see if he can latch on to some smelling salts or *sal volatile*." Quickly, she rolled Wolosyk over on his back, deftly loosened his shirt collar, and began slapping at his wrists, pinching the cheeks.

Now there, thought Barr, are the makings of a Grade-A nurse. Fast responses, good judgment, cool detachment—but did she also have the mental capacity and long range stamina she would need to fully overcome her handicaps of sex and color to make it as a Grade-A doctor?

As for Wolosyk, Barr had misgivings. Fainting, or syncope due to cerebral anoxia, was not unusual among medical students witnessing their very first big operation, for example, but any beginning intern should long since be sufficiently inured to blood and death. Emotional disturbance was certainly involved here but not likely to be the sole cause of the intern's vasomotor instability. Possibly there were contributing and even more serious factors—hypertension, cerebral arteriosclerosis, carotid sinus reflex, drug poisoning—any number of abnormal states that could adversely affect doctor capabilities. He would require a series of tests for Wolosyk and keep a close watch on his future behavior.

Meanwhile Kloster had started toward the black girl with a water pitcher. "You'll find we have a well-equipped hospital, Doctor," he said, smiling. "Try a little of this H_2O, and if that doesn't bring him around, we'll administer a bit of phenyleprine."

Briefly, Barr watched as the girl sprinkled water on the face of Wolosyk, who was beginning to stir.

"Our colleague appears to be in very capable hands,"

he observed wryly, and started away. "The rest of you will now follow me and we'll look in on a few more of the patients who were not so fortunate . . ."

four

Leaving the administration building—where, by hospital rules, all the medical staff was required to check in—Dr. Adam Cane strode through the enclosed atrium garden toward the Children's Pavilion. Surrounded as it was on four sides by buildings preoccupied with sickness and death, the garden was intended as a pleasant oasis of peace and charm. The gift of an automobile magnate, it had been designed by an internationally famed landscape architect and was replete with exotic flowers, lush shade trees, rich green lawn, and in the center, a large fountain consisting of three bronze female nudes in graceful positions squirting from discreet parts of their anatomies glistening streams of water that rose high in the air and created delicate rainbows under the bright morning sun. One of them reminded him of Ilse Jensen, and for a few moments an unbidden sensory playback of the blonde nurse's charms flooded his memory cells, accompanied by a warm gush of eroticism.

Angrily, Adam forced the enticing vision from his mind and hastened his steps. Nearly forty-five minutes had elapsed since the phone call to Ilse's apartment concerning the VSD patient going into heart failure—forty-five minutes too many in a heart case where each passing second could weigh heavily against the hairline balance between life and death. The first hour after a heart seizure was the most crucial; either the patient died or—with proper treatment—was generally considered over the hump.

Fortunately, the patient would be in good hands: Dr. Don Wolff, Chief Resident—and nominally an assistant to Adam—was an able pediatric cardiologist.

Dr. Wolff was seated beside the bed of eleven year old Holly Robbins talking in a soothing voice when Adam entered the patient's semi-private room, which was large and gaily decorated with bright wall murals. Private endowment money had been poured lavishly into the new Children's Pavilion, making it the showplace of the hospital, and even the poorest of pediatric patients were provided with pleasant quarters.

"Hello, Dr. Cane," Holly greeted brightly. "Did you hear what happened to me? I had everybody around here worried for awhile!"

Relieved, Adam smiled at the extraordinarily pretty girl. For some inexplicable reason, it seemed that nearly all "heart babies"—those born with a serious heart defect—had an exquisite, other-worldly kind of beauty. Her body, although small for her age and very thin—due to the deformed heart—was graceful, and she had large luminous eyes deep-set in a delicate face in which every feature was cameo-perfect.

"I was worried, too, Holly. That's why I'm here."

"Well, the little crisis is over," said Wolff in a genial, booming voice. He was a burly man of medium height with piercing dark eyes and a scrub brush head of short black hair. "Holly is doing just fine, aren't you, honey?"

"I'm feeling okay now, but gee, you should have seen me when my heart started jumping, Dr. Cane. I bet the whole bed was shaking. I would have fainted, I guess, if Dr. Wolff hadn't come in time to put that thingamajig against my chest—" she pointed to the electric "paddle" apparatus nearby, which told Adam the rest of the story. Holly's heart had gone into fibrillation, or arrhythmia—a dangerous irregularity of the heartbeat that could kill. To counter this, the electric paddle was used to jolt the fibrillating heart with enough current to send it back to fairly normal rhythm.

Looking at her merry young face, it was plain that Holly had no awareness of how closely she had brushed against death—nor a full realization of the grave condition of her diseased heart. The VSD, or ventricular septal defect, with which she had been born was a whopping hole in her septum—the partition that separates the two ventricles of the lower chambers of the heart. From the time of her birth, this had caused the right ventricle to work furiously, pumping blood into the lungs for oxygenation while at the same time fighting off pressure from the left ventricle. The overworked heart, beating so much harder than it should have, had kept enlarging as surely as the muscles on a man's arm enlarges when he lifts heavy weights every day, until now it crowded her entire chest cavity.

"It prickled like a thousand little needles," she chattered on, "but I didn't mind because I'm used to getting all kinds of needles stuck into me."

"You were very brave, honey," said Wolff, patting her hand.

"How is the potassium level, Don?"

"It was down to 3.1. I injected enough to bring it up close to 4." An even 4 was normal.

"Is potassium a vitamin?" said Holly. "Wasn't I getting enough vitamins?"

Adam smiled. "It's a little like that, Holly. Potassium is one of the chemical agents in your blood—we call them electrolytes—that controls heart rhythm."

"Gee, I've been going to so many doctors all my life, I'm getting to learn everything about medicine. Maybe I'll be a doctor when I grow up—so you better do a good job of fixing up my sick heart. How long do I have to wait before you can operate?"

"That's hard to say, Holly. We've still got a lot of tests to take, and of course, the final decision is up to Dr. Strang."

She wrinkled her pretty brow. "That's funny—when I asked Dr. Strang the same question this morning, he didn't answer me."

Adam shot a surprised glance at Wolff, who nodded briefly, then said to Holly, "You've got to realize that Dr. Strang is a very busy man, Holly, preoccupied with endless important duties. He probably didn't even hear you."

"I don't think so. I bet he's just shy around pretty girls." She giggled. "You tell him I'll forgive him this time—" she waggled a finger at both doctors—the imperious princess giving orders to her devoted lackeys—"but if he doesn't get hustling on my operation, I'll be very angry at him. Now be sure and tell him."

Wolff laughed. "Don't worry, honey. We're going to fix you up just as soon as possible. But for now, no more talk. Dr. Cane and I have many things to discuss. Meanwhile, anything you want, just ask the nurse."

Going out, Wolff closed the door behind them and after a short distance down the corridor said quietly, "The kid's really in trouble, Adam. I think I heard a leak today that wasn't there yesterday. My guess is a deteriorating mitral valve torn loose."

"Christ, I hope you're wrong." Holly's VSD problem

was bad enough in itself. Although the majority of such operations were successful, in Holly's case the disease had gone on too long. The heart was too bloated, the hole too large. Many top heart surgeons wouldn't risk it. And if on top of that, a valve had to be repaired, Holly's chances were all but hopeless.

"I can't be absolutely certain, of course," said Wolff, "without doing another cath—and I sure as hell hate to put the kid through that again."

A "cath", or heart catheterization, had been done on Holly only yesterday—the second one in her young life. The technique was to insert a heart catheter—a plastic-encased wire tube about the size of very thin spaghetti with special monitoring capabilities—into a vein of an arm or the groin and work it up through the vein until it reached the heart. Anesthesia made the procedure painless, and the movement of the catheter could be directed precisely by X-ray—in effect, giving the doctor a set of eyes within the heart itself with which to examine the damage as well as gain other data such as heart blood pressure and oxygen content readings.

Remembering, Adam felt gloom. Yesterday, gently pushing the catheter at the incision in Holly's arm while guiding its passage over a television screen, he had been shocked as he watched the wire move murkily into the shadow that was the heart. The shadow was enormous, evil.

Later, Wolff had commented, "My God, it's so malformed, the cath just flopped from side to side."

"It's a mess," Adam agreed. "The heart's just too big for her body."

"The mystery to me is how she lived long enough to get here. Frankly, I'll be surprised if Strang can do anything for her."

"That remains to be seen."

Thereafter, Adam had rushed through the tests that

had to be completed before an operation. Holly was given a new physical examination, a new set of chest X-rays was made, also a specimen of urine taken for analysis and a sample of blood for a CBC—a complete blood count. This was a count of red cells, the white cells, an estimate of the hemoglobin (oxygen-carrying pigment of the red cells) and an estimate of the hematocrit, or total proportion of solid matter in the blood—red cells plus the white cells—as well as a check on the ability of the blood to clot. Holly had arrived yesterday morning, on an emergency basis, and by late afternoon after the catheterization had been done, Dr. Strang had not yet seen her, but Adam had no doubt that the famed heart specialist—who had successfully done many VSD operations in the past— would give highest priority to squeezing Holly into his already crowded operating schedule.

And now, with the added possibility of a torn heart valve, Adam was even more certain that there was not a moment to be lost.

"I don't think there's any need for another cath, Don," he told the Chief Resident. "I think we'd better proceed on the assumption that Strang will want to get her on the table as soon as possible—and once we get her chest open, we'll know the full story."

Wolff shook his head worriedly. "Just be prepared for the probability that there won't be an operation, Adam. Strang stopped in just long enough to look over the X-rays and the cath films. He didn't deign to honor me with his opinion, but if I'm any judge of the involuntary nuances of expression, it's thumbs down on this case."

"That's reading one hell of a lot into one mere non-expression," Adam said, thinking of Strang's usual medical poker face.

"Adam, we don't have to bullshit each other. Strang's lost his balls, and you know it. He's no longer willing to stick his neck out on the really tough ones—but I have to be even more blunt and say this is one case where I'd tend to agree with him if he comes to a negative decision."

Adam stared at him in astonishment. "You mean you're not in favor of the operation?"

"If I were the surgeon on the case, I wouldn't touch her."

"But yesterday—"

"Yesterday I kidded myself into thinking there was a slight, a *very* slight chance. Today, with more of the facts in, I'm convinced she'd die on the table. She simply has no heart reserve left."

"Then what in the hell *would* you do with her, Don?"

Wolff turned away, embarrassed. "Just pass the buck, I guess—maybe send her to the Cleveland or Houston clinics. Let somebody else send her home to die."

"Well, we'll soon find out," Adam said tightly. "I'm going in to see Strang now." Angry, he swung around and started away.

"I almost forgot—" the Chief Resident called after him. "You'll probably find Holly's parents waiting at your office. I sent them there because I haven't the necessary, uh—finesse to tell them the whole truth about their kid. That's going to be your unenviable job."

". . . and about the suitcase, Miss Kozak," the detective was saying, "how heavy would you say it was?"

He paused in his pacing to again stare directly into Nurse Kerri Kozak's eyes, which for some odd reason stirred her with vague little quivery feelings she couldn't identify. They were really remarkable eyes, she thought. Of bluish grey, deep and earnest, and at the same time seeming to penetrate, like laser rays, through all her bones and flesh to the innermost, secret parts of her.

"I'm sorry, Mr. Lon—I mean, Detective London. I only moved it a couple times and I didn't really notice." For the past fifteen minutes, seated on the lounge in the small anteroom outside of the Supervisor of Nurses' office, Kerri had been answering questions about the deceased, Karl Lentz, and the black man, William "Speed" Wilson—about anything she may have overheard spoken between the two, the time of Wilson's departure, and so forth. Silly questions that made little sense, it seemed to her.

"Would you say it was heavy or light?"

"I'd have to say it was heavy."

"Can you be a little more specific—like if it was full of rocks, for example, or more like packed with telephone books?"

She looked away and scrunched her forehead in a pretense of deep thought—really only as an excuse to break the hypnotic grip of his eyes. She had read somewhere that the inability to look back into another's eyes denoted guilt, and she certainly didn't want the detective to think she had anything to feel guilty about. It was just that the impact of his probing glances made her feel captive and helpless, like a bird unable to fly from a stalking cat.

"I guess more like telephone books," she said.

"Thank you, Miss Kozak. I guess that about covers it for now, and I certainly appreciate your cooperation." He smiled and again looked earnestly, deeply into her eyes, adding, "but in case there are other questions we might have to ask—I mean, like after your usual working hours—where can we get in touch with you, just for the records?"

She was aware her heart was beating too fast, and another quivery little thrill went down her spine. Before she could answer, Miss Clugg opened the door of her inner office and peered out sternly.

"Miss Kozak can be reached at any time, night or day," she told the officer, "by calling either me or the night supervisor of nurses."

The nosy old bat, Kerri thought resentfully as she got up to leave. She had just begun enjoying the questioning, dumb as it was. The young detective wasn't all that handsome, but good-looking enough in a hard kind of way, and she liked the way he walked—kind of powerful and springy, on the balls of his feet, like maybe a prize fighter or a tiger. But it was those eyes that got to her.

"In case you remember anything else," he called after her, "you can always reach me at police headquarters. Just ask for Detective Jerry London."

Jerry London, Jerry London. She'd remember that.

Although the white-tiled corridors and rooms of the Pathology Department in the basement were by far the coolest part of the hospital, Mike Tunstra was beginning to sweat. Not from excessive exertion—of which the scraggly-haired orderly had never been guilty—but because in just a few more moments the suspenseful curiosity that had been plaguing him since last night would be ended. A few minutes ago, the Path Chief had been called over to the Administration Building, whereupon the black *diener*, Clem Jackson, had seized the opportunity to take off for a coffee break (inviting Mike to come, but Mike had declined).

And now, finally alone in the somber silence of the chambers of the dead, Mike hustled back to the little alcove housing two rows of lockers used by the orderlies and maintenance men in the basement wing. Quickly, he got his locker open, bent to paw aside a crumpled heap of hospital whites ready for laundering, and lifted out the black leather traveling bag that had been concealed beneath.

Mike had obtained the black bag by pure chance—plus Mike's opportunist wits. Last night he had taken over Emergency Room duty for another orderly, Denny Klarr, who had something going with a nurse whose only night free for the whole week was on that particular night. Since most of the orderlies, including Mike, sooner or later were required to go on night duty, on a revolving basis, it was expedient to have a stand-in arrangement for those nights when personal matters were more pressing than work.

The first couple hours had been dull: the usual mothers with snot-nosed babies suffering anything from measles to turning blue from something they swallowed, a teen-age girl fearful that her skin rash was VD, an old guy in cardiac arrest rushed in from a nursing home, an old bag with a hangnail that kept her from sleeping, a sobbing hysterical skinny chick with slashed wrists that turned out to be just "hesitation marks"—razor scratches too shallow to lose much blood, a fake suicide attempt to get attention. That kind of crap. An intern and one of the resident doctors—"on call" if needed—shoved them through as fast as possible with the help of one orderly and two nurses, one of them being the EW Admissions nurse who did all she could to hold up the works with detailed, fussy paperwork.

And then shortly after dark there had been a tumultuous entry—a girl rushing in, a black girl with a tumbleweed mass of hair and long brown legs that seemed to just keep going on up, up, endlessly before vanishing beneath a wisp of micro-mini skirt.

"Quick—!" she called out to nobody in particular. "They's a man outside, he all shot up an' dyin'!"

The intern on duty, Chris Holland, looked up from his copy of *Playboy* in boredom. This was his very last day of the internship year as a provisionally practicing doctor—tomorrow he would be a full-fledged M.D.

"Roll out the stretcher," he snapped at Mike in an imperious manner, perhaps unconsciously, but already seeming a bit puffed with the great new aura of author-ity and respect that would be his due on the morrow.

Resentfully, Tunstra pushed the stretcher out. Under the hospital floodlights he saw the black girl had gone on ahead to a low-slung yellow Stingray and opened a door.

"This is him," she called, pointing inside, and then, oddly, turned and began running.

From behind, Holland called, "Hey you—come back here!" But the long legs only kept flashing with re-flected highlights until she vanished into outer darkness.

"That crazy chick," said Holland. "Why do you sup-pose she did that?"

Mike shrugged contemptuously. "Who knows?" Any dope ought to be able to figure out the broad was prob-ably a hooker with a record or had a jealous husband at home and couldn't afford to get involved.

Holland peered into the front of the car. "Look, I'll haul him out this side by the legs and you get in from the other side and get a good grip under the arms."

Yeah, the bloody end of him, Mike thought with in-creasing resentment as he climbed in as ordered and saw that the black face of the moaning man, slumped low on the front seat, was purplish with dribbling blood and the fancy pink ruffled shirt as well as the front of the man's canary jacket, Edwardian style, were a gory mess. A snazzy dresser, Mike conceded grudgingly. The striped, flared pants, polished boots, the sparkle of a diamond ring—everything boasted, "Look—I'm loaded."

It was while helping move him out that Mike hap-pened to glance back and see the black bag on the floor. His instant guess was that it would probably con-

tain, along with the fancy duds, a couple bottles of
booze, a few lids of good grass, a supply of poppers,
maybe even some reserve bread stashed under the lin-
ings.

By the time they got the wounded man on the
stretcher, Mike's opportunist instincts—never able to
resist an angle that might lead effortlessly to any kind
of unearned goodies—had taken over.

"Look, you roll him in, Doc," he said in an authori-
tative tone fueled by his greedy haste. "I got strict orders from the Administrator to make sure no vehicles
obstruct this driveway."

Before the nonplused Holland could object, Mike
piled into the car and slammed the driver's door
shut—noting with a kind of queasy fascination that the
window glass had been shattered into a pattern of bursting stars around a series of bullet holes. Revving up
the motor, he roared off like an entrant in the Grand
Prix. Exultant. So what the hell, Holland would be
leaving tomorrow for a residency somewhere, or into
private practice to get fat and rich. Mike often sim-
mered with bitterness at the unfairness of it. He had a
better brain than half the doctors he knew but somehow had got stuck with being just another half-ass orderly to kick around.

At the far end of the spacious parking lot out of
sight from the hospital entrance, he parked and got out
on the shadowed side of the vehicle with the bag—man
it was *heavy*—then hustled across to a side hospital entry to the basement. Fortunately, the morgue was
empty of life and he was able to make it to his locker
unseen, hide the bag, and hurry back to EW where nobody had missed him because Holland and one nurse
were busy in the shock room with the wounded man
while the Admissions nurse was in a flurry of excitement trying to call the resident doctor and the police on
two phones at the same time.

The troopers and cluster of policemen, when they arrived, only added to the confusion. It had got out, somehow, that the black man was Speed Wilson, who was mixed up with the Mafia in the numbers racket. They couldn't question him because he was already in a coma, and the doctors had nothing to say except report on his condition. Finally they got around to Mike:

"You say the person who drove him here was a black female?"

"Yeah."

"Young?"

"Could be. I didn't get too good a look at her before she flaked off like a bat out of hell."

"How would you describe her?"

"Christ officer, like I said, I was too busy doing my job to take down notes for you guys. She looked—you know, just like any of them."

"Took off in a hurry, hunh? Carrying anything?"

"I didn't notice." Mike had a belated thought. "But come to think of it, she did run kind of funny, like she could be holding a baby or a package or something in front of her."

"You sure of that?"

Mike looked dubious. By this time he knew he was onto something real hot. The numbers racket wasn't Mickey Mouse shit. Each runner raked in thousands in collection money every day, and Speed Wilson straw-bossed them all—right up there next to the big juice. It made his brain spin just thinking of what might be in that bag.

"Nah . . ." he said, shaking his head. He regretted being so quick in trying to plant the idea—in case the cops somehow found out a bag was missing—that the black girl had snatched it. You try to be too helpful, it always boomeranged. "I guess it could have been just high heels that made her run, you know—kind of wild and floppy."

"Wearing high heels, hunh?"

"I don't *know* she was wearing high heels—it was just a guess. Use your head, officer—here I am loading a half-dead guy on a stretcher—have I got time to look that close at a broad's legs?"

The cop, a paunchy sergeant, looked up from the pad he was scribbling on and gave Mike a sharp brief glance. "Not you, buddy, not you."

"If you don't mind," Mike said huffily, "I'd like to get back to my job. I've told you everything I know."

"You're the guy who moved the car, aren't you?"

"I was just following my orders to keep the entrance drive outside of EW cleared at all times."

"Show me where you parked it."

With the sergeant and two other cops trailing along, he led them out to the Stingray in the visitors' parking lot.

"Way back here, hunh?" The sergeant's glance skimmed around the near-empty lot. "Seems to me there's plenty of space a lot closer to the entrance."

"I knew it wouldn't be picked up for a few days, so I got it as far out of the way as possible. Man, this place gets like a madhouse with visitors' cars during the day."

"Did you notice anything in the car—like a box or package of any kind?"

"Not a thing. I'm no damned snoop. Do you mind if I go now, officer?"

"First, give me your home address and phone, Mr. Tunstra. We might have some more questions later."

Mike told him sullenly, meanwhile noting that the other cops were peering in, around, and under the car. One lifted the hood; the other opened a door and climbed into the backseat.

"Would you mind telling me what this is all about, officer?"

"Read the papers, buddy," said the sergeant, turning

away, "then divide it by two and multiply by bullshit and you'll know as much about it as I do."

Back in EW, Mike got increasingly nervous. His original plan had been to slip back down to his locker at the first opportune moment, strip the bag of any valuables (hiding the loot in a bundle of soiled laundry) and then stuff the suitcase down the hospital incinerator. As it turned out, he was kept too busy in EW, and when finally the relief orderly arrived at about midnight and he was free to go down to the locker room, he faced another problem. Several goldbricking orderlies had started a poker game on the bench between the locker rows. Mike's alternate idea, which was to sneak the suitcase out of a side basement door and lug it way to hellengone around to his own car in the employees' parking lot behind the old hospital building—a risky plan at best, with so many pigs around—had to be abandoned.

Which turned out to be a lucky break, because his heap was stopped by a police car at the end of the driveway from the hospital and two of the pigs did a thorough job of shaking it down—poking around in the trunk, under the seats, everywhere—before waving him on.

Perspiring, Mike worked diligently with a hammer and screwdriver, and being no novice at forcing cheap locks, had little trouble in getting the suitcase open— only to be rewarded by a sudden, sinking disappointment.

Instead of the wads of pretty green currency he had been so sure would be stuffed inside, the suitcase was tightly packed with about a dozen largish transparent plastic bags full of white stuff that could have been sugar—but wasn't. The truth hit him with an even greater jolt than his first shock of disappointment.

Heroin.

That made everything fall into place—the shooting, the black chick's vanishing act, all the fuss and furor of so many troopers and cops and probably an army of plainclothes narcs. There'd never been much police pressure on the numbers racket—particularly since the new legalized lottery got started in the state—but efforts to crack the big drug rings had intensified. Mike was an avid reader of crime news and was well aware—and even a little proud of the fact—that drug addiction in Detroit and its surrounding suburbs had mushroomed to the number one highest per capita rate in the whole country—way ahead of New York and Chicago—and so was the crime rate. The Jones men—"Jones" being black ghetto slang for both heroin and the habit—had taken over a large part of Motor City as their private turf, hauling in overnight fortunes and spreading to other towns. All the police departments in lower Michigan had been beefed up to try and stop it.

Mike stared at the plastic bags with little tingles of apprehension slithering down his spine. His attitude toward drugs in general was "liberal"—now and then he blew a little grass, and had experimented with its more potent form as hash (which made him too hyper, so he'd dropped it)—but horse really scared him. He'd seen enough OD cases brought into the hospital to give anybody nightmares. So now what the Christ was he going to do with it?

Approaching footsteps sent his already jittering nerves into a new tizzy. Hastily he closed the suitcase and shoved it back into the locker and slammed the door shut.

five

In Adam's small office, Holly's parents sat nervous and ill at ease. Fred Robbins, a husky but fattening man in his mid-forties, leaned forward with elbows on his knees and work-seamed hands clasped together.

"You don't have to pull any punches with us, Doctor. We want the true facts, no matter how bad—right, Elsa?" He glanced at the thin woman beside him.

Elsa Robbins, haggard, dowdy, eyes reddened from recent crying, nodded and smiled tremulously. "We've lived with it for a long time, and keep praying for the best, so I guess we're as ready as we'll ever be to face up to the worst."

Adam appraised the harried couple soberly. How encouraging could he be without raising false hopes? How honest without crushing them? "First, let me make it clear that anything I say is only a personal opinion. I haven't as yet had an opportunity to consult with Dr. Strang, and his opinion could differ."

"That's okay with us. We were told you could answer any questions about Holly and the operation they say she should have. On the level, Doctor—what are the chances of pulling through this kind of operation?"

"There's no simple answer. This is high-risk surgery. In the majority of such operations, we've been successful, but in Holly's case . . ."

Adam hesitated, not wanting to add to their anguish by saying they'd waited too long. A year or two sooner, even a few months ago, might have made all the difference. It wasn't their fault, of course. Shortly after birth, their family doctor had detected a murmur. "I've heard these before," he told the worried parents, "and my educated guess is there's nothing to worry about." A year later she'd fallen, gasping for breath, lips turning blue, and was rushed into an oxygen tent. The cardiologist had put her on digitalis—one tablet a day—to slow her fast heart and strengthen it. At three, following a similar episode, she was taken to a big city hospital for her first heart catheterization, which revealed the suspected VSD. The Robbins were advised to wait until she was older and stronger for the open heart surgery that she would eventually need. As time passed, they began to hope the doctor was wrong. Although unable to play like normal children, Holly was bright and happy enough, and by carefully protecting her from exertions beyond her capacity, she seemed to be doing fine.

Until the past couple months, when Holly had fainted several times—something she'd never done before—and then last week had collapsed with the worst seizure yet, turning bluish, choking for breath, cold sweat on her forehead—in classic heart failure. Again she was rushed into an oxygen tent in the nearest hospital, where the staff cardiologist persuaded the Robbins to get her to the Tri-County heart clinic for observation as soon as possible.

"You realize, of course," Adam went on, "that the hole in her heart has been there since birth, and it's . . .

pretty bad." There was no point, he decided, in revealing the monstrous size of the heart, how big the hole, how extremely difficult the procedure of stitching into flabby heart muscle the large Dacron patch that would be needed to repair it—nor how greatly the risk would be increased if Dr. Wolff's suspicion of a torn heart valve proved correct.

"Would you say she has a fifty-fifty chance, Doctor?"

"I'm afraid it's far less than that. You see, it's not just the hole in the septum—I think that can be fixed—but there could be unforeseen complications. And even assuming that such an operation went perfectly, with no complicating factors, there's still a greater problem to worry about—that's the three or four days later. In major surgery of this kind, there's no certainty that Holly's body will have the strength to recover."

Elsa Robbins lowered her head and began to weep soundlessly.

"I'm sorry if I've been too blunt, Mrs. Robbins. I just wanted to be sure you understand the risks are high. Very high."

"With the odds that bad," Fred Robbins voice was hoarse, "maybe it'd be better if we just took her home, and—I mean, hope for the best and keep her happy for as long as, you know . . ."

It was a cruel dilemma for the parents—whether to keep the merry but sickly child at home and crowd all the time left with love, or risk her to an operation with only the bleakest hopes of success.

"The choice is clear. Either you consider surgery— or take her home and wait. It wouldn't be long. Her decline is very rapid. She simply has no heart reserve left—it can no longer rally on demand to produce more output for such simple exertions as climbing stairs, for example, or to fight infections. If she caught a cold, it could be a catastrophe. Even if she stumbled over a toy, or merely sneezed, she could go out like a light."

Fred Robbins' eyes swam, spilled over. He turned his head away, ashamed, and got out a handkerchief and loudly blew his nose.

"Would you care for a glass of water and a sedative, Mr. Robbins?"

"No, thanks. I'll be okay. Just tell me one thing, Doctor—would you operate on her if she was your kid?"

"I certainly wouldn't want to—but I would."

Elsa Robbins dabbed at her eyes with a Kleenex. "If you think there's any chance, only a tiny chance, then I guess Fred and I are ready to put her in your hands and the Lord's."

"As I mentioned earlier, there's a possibility that Dr. Strang will not agree with my opinion. He's the one who makes the final decision concerning all operations."

"How soon will we know for sure?"

"Check back with my office this afternoon. By then, I should have the final word."

Kerri Kozak's confused thoughts about her reactions to Detective Jerry London (along with vague stirrings in her visceral area) were short-lived. As she was passing one of the semi-private rooms adjacent to the Recovery Room, an eruption of odd noises from within startled her back to the present.

Looking in, she saw the commotion was being caused by old Bart Smith, an agile little old man of eighty-four, who despite bandages around his midsection and the dangling tubes of monitoring machines—some of them already torn loose—was hopping around on his bed emitting squawks of outrage.

". . . no, no, *no*—" he was squawking, "not me you don't! I know what you got in mind."

Nurse Nelda Frey, a somewhat chunky little redhead, was waltzing around the bed endeavoring to snatch the old fellow's legs but he kept nimbly hopping out of reach. Seeing Kerri, she beckoned urgently.

"He's gone squirrely," she said. "Get on the other side of the bed and we'll corner him."

Kerri circled the bed gingerly. "What am I supposed to—?"

"Just *grab*—and whatever you get, hold on tight."

Together they managed to grasp him by both legs, and surprisingly he offered no resistance as they gently forced him back down to a recumbent position.

"Would you believe it?" said Nelda. "An eighty-four year old man acting like a spoiled brat! He's been driving me up the walls."

"I'm sure Mr. Smith doesn't quite realize how he's behaving."

"I know. When they're a little senile it takes a lot longer for the sedations and anesthesia to wear off. It really scrambles their brains."

"What was he operated on for?"

"He only had his gall bladder taken out—but the way he's been carrying on, you'd think it was his penis." She handed Kerri a furry white stay. "Take this and strap that arm down and I'll get this one . . ."

While they were putting his arms in restraint, old Bart had begun sobbing and kicking his legs like a child in a tantrum.

"I really don't know what to do next," said Nelda, exasperated. "Do me a favor, Kerri, and keep an eye on him while I find a doctor." As she turned to go, the old fellow managed to twist his torso to the side of the bed and delivered a rabbity kick against Nelda's ample posterior.

She whirled, eyes blazing. "All right, you old

nuisance—that really *does* it! Now I'm going to strap down both your legs, and put a gag in your mouth if I have to!"

Sobbing, the patient turned beseeching eyes toward Kerri. "Don't let her hogtie me," he begged.

Kerri smiled at the wet, wrinkled old face. "Perhaps Miss Frey will change her mind if you promise to behave, Mr. Smith."

"I won't kick her no more," he said.

Nelda shrugged. "We'll see what the doctor has to say . . ." She backed off cautiously and went out.

Old Bart at once ceased his sobbing and beckoned Kerri to come closer. "Miss . . ." he said hoarsely, "you help me break outta this place an' I'll give you my whole farm—a hundert an' twenty acres prime bottomland on the Tittabawassee River with the house, two barns, fourteen cows, all good Guernsey stock, a threshin' combine—the whole shebang—an' marry you to boot. I could show you a better time than any young squirt you ever dreamed about."

"I'm very flattered, Mr. Smith, but when you're in such a fine hospital getting the best of possible care, why are you so anxious to leave?"

"I'm nobody's fool, Miss—" he peered around slyly and continued in a frightened whisper, "This end of the hospital is the spare parts department—this is where they keep you for experiments, an' then sell the extra pieces for big prices to rich folks who need new parts. That smart-ass nurse and them doctors are in it together makin' a fortune, an' you'd better believe it."

Kerri knew that in the post-operative phase, some elderly patients—already confused by drugs not yet dispelled from their systems—became paranoid, full of weird suspicions.

"Now whatever gave you such a silly idea?" she said, restraining an impulse to add that she doubted that anyone would care to buy any of his spare parts.

"They already took all my innards out. I can't feel nothing left down there."

"Only your gall bladder was removed, Mr. Smith."

"That's what *they* say. I know better because I can feel there's a lot more missin'."

"I'm sure that if you ask the doctor, he can explain—"

A male voice intruded. "Now what seems to be the problem here?" Dr. Melton Kloster had arrived with Nelda Frey beside him.

"The patient is still disoriented," said Nelda. "Unless I keep him in restraint, he jumps around and shouts and disturbs the whole ward."

Kloster grinned. "It sometimes happens when the cardiac output fails. What have you given him?"

"Thorazine and Demerol, but it doesn't seem to help."

"How much Demerol?"

"Thirty-five milligrams."

"Give him another fifty."

Nelda looked startled. "That much for such an old man?"

"You've got a nuisance problem, right? That much Demerol, at worst, will only depress his blood pressure—and he sure as hell needs a little depressing before he kills himself."

"Whatever you say, Doctor."

For a few moments, Kloster watched the patient straining against the stays. "That old guy's got more ginger than I have," he said before turning to go. "You can make book on it—he's one that's going to walk out of here on his own two feet . . ."

After he was gone, Kerri said, "Do you still need me, Nelda?"

"I can handle him now, Kerri. Thanks."

As Kerri turned she felt a thudding impact against

her derriere. She whirled, momentarily furious. "Mr. *Smith*! You promised you wouldn't do that again!"

Old Bart stretched his mouth into a roguish grin. "I only said I wouldn't kick *her* no more."

six

When, from behind her tidy desk in the anteroom outside of the surgical director's office, Glenna Woods saw Adam approaching, her repressed, smouldering feelings of wounded love and outraged pride flared into momentary hate.

She could forgive him for standing her up—even, for dating another woman—but when the other woman was Ilse Jensen, the hospital super sex symbol, she could never hope to compete.

Not that Glenna lacked female charms. With her taffy-brown hair, clear hazel eyes set in a pleasant face, and tallish neat figure, she was typical of the wholesome, all-American girl seen in so many TV commercials with an aura of untouchable "niceness"— which wasn't entirely true, although quite a number of disappointed males who had dated her considered her impossibly prudish.

The truth was that she was simply very discriminat-

ing, incapable of giving her body to a man with whom
she was not in love.

That had happened only three times. The first, a col-
lege romance, withered away soon after her lover split
from the establishment to join a sleazy commune. The
next one was shipped off to Viet Nam, where that Big
Love died suddenly two years later—not nobly and
dramatically from a battlefield death, but far worse,
from a humiliating "Dear Jane" letter contritely advis-
ing her that he was bringing home a Vietnamese bride.

The last and by far the most important was Dr.
Adam Cane, so perfectly epitomizing the "Mr. Right"
of her dreams that she had stubbornly discounted his
frank warning, early in their dating, that he had no intention of getting married. A good doctor, he
maintained, could only be married to his profession.

She had accepted him on these terms, confident that
with time and wiles and persistence she could prove to
him that he needed her as much as she needed him. And
had thought she was succeeding—until last night . . .

"Glenna—"

She finished a line of careful typing before looking
up, wishing to register her vast disinterest as well as to
better organize the lofty, cool demeanor with which she
wanted to confront him.

"Oh yes, Dr. Cane . . ." she said lightly, giving him
the bright but clinically impersonal smile reserved for
visitors and menials. "Dr. Strang has been expecting
you. I'll let him know you're here . . ." She reached to
press the intercom button.

"That can wait, Glenna. First, I'd like to explain
about last night . . ."

Last night! And to think that less than a week ago,
she had lain hot, naked and throbbing with love in his
arms. *Totally* his. Again the hate—a bitter pressure—
rose to her throat and came out sugar-coated venom:

"No need to apologize. I perfectly understand that you had more . . . interesting plans."

"But it's not that way at all——"

She had pressed the button. A red light winked on. "Dr. Cane is here to see you, Dr. Strang."

"Have him come right in," came the immediate response.

Adam waited until she had snicked the OFF button. "Perhaps we can meet later for a talk, Glenna."

"I'm terribly sorry, Dr. Cane, but I——"

Before she could finish he swung away, and strode into the surgical director's office.

She had a wild desire to bite her tongue until she screamed. Instead, her fingers furiously tapped out a staccato burst of typing—making two errors, which only made her madder.

In the fourth floor conference room, Dr. Barr flicked on the switch of one of the X-ray view boxes and turned to smile at the assemblage of interns.

"Perhaps it will help alleviate your obvious weariness and boredom," he said amiably, "if we now indulge in a bit of armchair doctoring—that is, X-ray diagnosis. The film I have just illuminated, as you will note, is a chest X-ray, but before we examine it in detail, let me give you the history of the patient."

Barely listening to the droning voice of the medical director, Steve Wolosyk sat brooding at the rear of the group. The shame of fainting in front of others—especially embarrassing, he thought wryly, for a husky big Polack bred to the code of male toughness, male supremacy—still lingered.

One reason for his unmanly weakness he attributed to the fact that he had been skimping on sleep for weeks—only two hours the previous night—and had also skipped breakfast.

But the main factor had been the emotional shock—the startling resemblance of the brain-dead kid in ICU to his own younger brother Ricky who, hopped up on speed or pot or whatever high he was on at the time, had killed himself in a wreck.

That plus the even crueler freak of coincident that had made him the one to pull the switch, that sped the brain-dead kid into complete death—a symbolic parallel to the role thrust upon him following their mother's death, and after the old man had taken to boozing it up every night, the responsibility to look after his much younger brother. A responsibility he had failed.

Over and beyond all that, Steve's present introspective mood was colored by that strange feeling, the fleeting vision during those dreamlike moments of regaining consciousness.

. . . a beautiful face, intensely familiar . . . The same sweet smile . . . a pervading sense of tender love . . . softness immutably fused with protective strength . . . his mother . . .

Then as the fog dispersed, he saw the face was black.

"Feeling better, Doctor?" she said briskly.

The vision was gone.

"What happened?" he said brusquely, and then remembering, looked around and was relieved to see that the other interns were gone and they were alone. "What the Christ are you doing here?"

His expression and tone of voice must have relayed only too clearly his bone-deep aversion toward black skin.

"Well, yo' seez, mistah," she countered with affected black ghetto dialect and a dazzling smile, "Ah jus' a kin'hearted lil ole uppity black *thang* from Geor'ja who lak tuh practice up m'd'cine on honkies 'til Ah gits good 'nough at it tuh use it on my soul brothers. Think yo' feel good 'nough, do yo', tuh pick up yo' lily white ass an' move it on down the hall aftah da others?"

He flushed, at first angry, then abashed, and got up clumsily. "No need for that goddamned chip on your shoulder."

"Look, Wolosyk, I'm from the inner 'Inner' City. My old man was a metal finisher in an auto plant and I grew up with my nose out of joint from smelling Duco lacquer and you Hamtramck Polacks fifteen miles away."

Steve, who had in fact grown up in Hamtramck, was puzzled. Hamtramck, sometimes referred to as "a city within a city" because it was surrounded by Detroit, was a 100% white community of about 26,000 Polish-Americans grimly determined to protect their cultural and religious heritage (and real estate values) by keeping it that way. Oddly enough, the main threat came from the federal government, with whom they were in continual, bitter battle due to government efforts to increase the construction of low and moderate income housing—which would open the gates to an influx of blacks from the bordering Negro community. Polish animosity toward the blacks was far more virulent than anything known in the deep South, matched only by the blacks' hatred of the Poles.

"How did you know?" he said. "Do I wear a brand or something?"

"It's just like the way a cat knows a dog when she sees one, Wolosyk."

He grinned. "I've been called lots worse by some of your soul brothers."

"You'd better believe it," she said dryly.

During this brief exchange, Steve became aware of a sensation he'd known only a few times before after meeting a particularly exciting girl—the suddenly ignited spark inside, steadily growing brighter. It wasn't that she was all that gorgeous, or loaded with the blatant sexuality ascribed by popular white myths to black females, but the high-cheekboned face over which the dark chocolate skin was stretched smooth and glistening as polished ebony had a distinctive kind of beauty that would have made a merely pretty girl beside her look cheap. Even the frizzly black hair which had always repelled him—at least, on Negro males—on her was stunning. She wore it in a subtle natural African hairdo—not the overdone Afro style of hair teased out about sixty miles in every direction until most of them looked like giant burnt cottonballs strutting around on legs—shaped close to her head like a thick cap. She was about five feet nine, he guessed. Tall, but still she had to tilt her head to look up at him. The intelligent bright eyes—brown with gold and black flecks—were amused and her moist full lips smiling.

"You look fully recovered, Doctor," she said mockingly, "so let's get on with the show."

Walking down the corridor, his awareness of her sleek dark body had intensified. Christ, she was really *built*. She exuded a musky perfume. Her movements were fluid—feline. He found himself trying to imagine what the feel of the silken ebony of her skin, the curves, would be like, and it made him physically ache.

All it proves, Wolosyk, he told himself savagely, is that you're just a horny, hotpants Polack. You can't get away from your own balls. Whenever you get a whiff of whatever damned chemistry it is that activates them, they leap all barriers, racial or otherwise.

"Wolosyk—!" The raised voice, like a cracking whip, jarred Steve back into the present. Dr. Barr was staring at him, half in annoyance, but also with concern. "You seem not to be listening. I trust you're medically informed enough to know whether you're in need of a physical examination—or just more sleep."

"I'm sorry, sir, but I've been following everything you've said," Steve lied.

Barr turned and again faced the illuminated X-ray in the view box.

"As I was saying ... this is a chest X-ray of a patient 42 years old, male, admitted six months ago complaining of unsteadiness and loss of balance. A neurological examination was made and failed to disclose any explanation for the symptoms. The only specific symptoms were his inability to maintain balance when he stood on one foot and nystagmus—an involuntary, jerky movement of the eyeballs when he looked out from the corners of his eyes. Unable to come up with a diagnosis, the neurologist sent him home, although it was known that something was wrong with his brain that couldn't be found.

"A few months later, the patient returned because his loss of balance was getting worse. This time, an electroencephalogram showed changes that suggested a mass lesion somewhere in the brain. Our neurologist now did a ventriculogram—a diagnostic procedure involving the introduction of air into the interior chambers of the brain that are normally filled with cerebrospinal fluid—and these studies revealed the outline of a brain tumor in an operable location. The skull was opened, and the large tumor peeled out so neatly it was believed to be benign—until pathology got a look at it and declared it was metastatic and looked suspiciously like brontogenic carcinoma.

"Of course, the patient was at once sent to X-ray for special new chest films—including stereos and sectional tomograms—and sure enough, a tiny tissue mass was discovered in the upper lobe of the left lung. It is well defined in the X-ray we are presently looking at—" Barr paused to indicate with a pencil the precise location of the cancerous growth—"so I want you all to come up to examine it closely and see for yourself what we're talking about."

Amid the sounds of shuffling feet—apathetic but

compliant—Steve rose up and joined the line of interns filing slowly past the X-ray. It was not that easy to see—only a soft shadow on the left lung—but certainly clear enough to any trained eyes.

"Now comes the part that really shakes us." Barr went on. "The brain operation took place six months after the patient's first admission into the hospital, at which time several chest films had been taken—all reported normal. Following the operation, our specialists got out the old chest films for a comparative examination, and this time—now knowing exactly where to look—were able to see the barest shadow of the beginning lesion that they had failed to spot six months earlier—at a time, I wish to stress, when it may very well have been operable before metastasizing to the brain. This is a further example of why I continue to emphasize the crucial—life and death—importance of accurate and timely diagnosis."

Turning, the medical director switched off the view box and turned on the one next to it, illuminating another chest X-ray similar to the first.

"This is one of the first films taken six months ago." Bending close, Barr studied it for a few moments, and then with a pencil pointed to a spot on the left lung— "Ah, yes, here it is . . . most difficult to see, but if you look carefully enough . . ." Again he faced the interns. "To emphasize the all-important art of properly using your eyes for accurate X-ray diagnosis, I suggest that all of you come up here, study the film thoroughly, and indicate to me whether you can see the shadow of the beginning lesion."

Steve waited while the others filed up to the view box and one by one, peered at it intently. Some nodded dubiously, some with conviction, murmuring affirmation to the effect that yes, they could see it. The black girl was now studying the film, and Steve went up to stand close behind her.

"If you say it's there, Dr. Barr," she said, "then it *must* be there—but to tell the truth, I'd hate to be the one responsible for finding it. I can see I'm going to need a lot of extra practice in reading X-rays."

"How about you, Wolosyk?" said Barr, a bit too harshly, Steve thought.

Resentfully, he looked long and hard at the lung area in question.

"I can't see a goddamned thing," he said after a few moments, knowing it was the wrong answer, but what the hell, if Barr was bent on making him the group scapegoat, he wasn't going to try and stop it by always agreeing and kissing the old bastard's paranoid ass.

Barr frowned. "Not a thing, Wolosyk? But everyone else—with the conditional exception of Dr. Wheeler— seem to have had no great difficulty in seeing the diseased area."

"All I saw was normal lung tissue," Steve said stubbornly. He saw the black girl, Wheeler, looking at him with a tiny, mocking smile.

"Wolosyk, I fear your future in medicine is going to be very hard and hazardous. While all of your contemporaries seated here, pleased and complacent, will be rolling in Cadillacs and mink-lined swimming pools, you'll still be sweating behind the medical plow, doing it the hard way." He beamed around at the interns. Some were fidgeting, uncertain.

"And that's the way it's got to be—" Barr's voice was suddenly angry, cracking out like a whip—"hard work and sweat. There is no easy road to medical excellence. Indeed, the way is strewn with heart-breaking obstacles, distractions, and fallacies, and even exotic diseases, often incurable, to which physicians are particularly susceptible—one of them being the ECS virus, which we have just witnessed in action."

The medical director paused, his face still flushed

from intensity of feeling, and went on in a more moderate tone:

"I have a confession to make. I played a little trick on you. The chest X-ray you just examined is of perfectly normal lungs. The only disease involved is the ECS virus that has infected all but two of you. I refer to the Emperor's Clothes Syndrome, an ailment first described by Hans Christian Andersen in 1837 and widespread among physicians today. A typical example of how it afflicts the unwary goes like this: a top-ranking doctor examines a patient and hears a faint heart murmur. The residents and interns accompanying him also listen and also hear the murmur—even when there is no murmur. It exists only in their faith that the master can't be wrong. The dangers are obvious. The disease can become chronic and the doctors suffering from it develop a dense hyper-immunity to the evidence of their own senses."

Barr turned and snicked off the view box and moving on, switched on the next two boxes, illuminating two new chest X-rays.

"We'll try again," he said wearily. "One of these is the film I misled you into thinking you were looking at—an X-ray of the patient taken six months ago. The other is not. Beginning with those in front, you will again come up here, one by one, and after your most careful study of both films, indicate to me in a whisper which one shows the very slight, almost imperceptible beginnings of brontogenic carcinoma. With the exception of Wolosyk and Wheeler, none of you will have my permission to leave this room until I am completely satisfied that all of you have used your God-given eyes to truly *see* what you are looking at."

As the first of the interns moved sheepishly toward the view boxes, Barr directed a benign smile at the black girl and Steve.

"Interns Wheeler and Wolosyk are now excused to

go directly to the bulletin board outside of my office, where you will find your assignments posted. You are expected to begin them without delay."

seven

At fifty-nine and still as slender as when twenty, Victor Strang was a handsome man. He had the ascetic, pale face of a saint, the icy-bright blue eyes of a fanatic, and the *hauteur* of an undisputed dictator—all of which he was, to some degree. A mane of once-blonde hair, now silvered, added to the aristocratic distinction of his appearance. It was all part of the invincible charisma with which he charmed women, awed patients, and intimidated members of his staff.

At the moment it was being exerted, full force, for the latter purpose.

"I am astonished, really astonished," he was saying to Adam Cane in a tone of strained patience, "that you should even *suggest* that we fit the VSD case into our operating schedule."

"But Vic, in view of the urgency—"

"Urgency? They're *all* urgent, Doctor! We have a woman going into OR-4—" he glanced at his watch— "in about forty-five minutes who has such extensive oc-

clusion of vessels in her left leg that gangrene has set
in. Right after that I'm doing a carotid—hopefully in
time to prevent another stroke—and after lunch, a
thoractomy, then a kidney transplant. And tomorrow—but you already know what we're facing. Our
back-up of OR cases—all of them urgent, God help
us—is so serious, we're having a problem just finding
holding space for them."

Adam, who would be assisting at all of the operations, knew each case fully as well as Strang did.

"Urgent, yes, but I consider the VSD to be an emergency." At Tri-County there were three categories of
OR cases, with considerable overlapping. Most crucial
was "emergency", requiring treatment within hours,
such as acute appendicitis, or internal hemorrhage.
Next in priority was "urgent", applied to cases that
were not quite an emergency but which the doctors did
not want to delay, as in suspected malignancy or gallstones that were causing intense pain. The third cate-
gory, "routine" was the catch-all for all cases that could
wait.

"—far more serious, for example," Adam went on,
"than the aneurysm we have scheduled for tomorrow
forenoon."

"An aneurysm, complicated by coronary ostial stenosis—and you consider it less serious!" exploded Strang.
It was almost a hospital cliche that having an aneurysm
was like sitting on a keg of dynamite with a lighted
fuse.

"As you recall, sir, the patient has managed to live
with his aneurysm for nearly two years without even
knowing he had it. It's a relatively stabilized lesion, and
since his admission, we've reduced the hypertension
and diffuse dilation. He's resting comfortably. The operation could just as well be delayed for a few days or
longer, with minimal risk. Whereas in the case of the
child—"

"Can I be hearing you correctly, Cane?" Strang's handsome features registered vast disbelief. "Are you suggesting that I change the operating sequence to displace Atlee Northrup—who happens to be the chairman of Amco Motors, an honorary member of the hospital board, and a dear friend of mine as well—displace *him* to make room for ... the offspring of some ignorant garage mechanic?"

"I did not mean precisely that, sir," Adam said coldly. "The disparity in the social and monetary standings of the two patients did not enter into my medical reasoning."

Strang flushed. As a rule he was scrupulously impartial in his treatment of the rich and the poor, different religions, different colors. However, having blundered into a remark that was highly unethical, even by his own standards, he was incapable of conceding error. His voice rose angrily:

"Your medical reasoning is so completely unrealistic that you utterly fail to grasp the main point, which is quite simple! The aneurysm is an *operable* case whereas this particular VSD case is most definitely not. When I looked over the cath films this morning I was appalled—*appalled*, Doctor, that you had not already advised the parents that it was hopeless and made appropriate arrangements for the patient to be removed from the hospital."

"May I submit, sir, that I cannot agree with your evaluation of the case as 'hopeless'."

"Since you obviously feel so much more qualified—" the surgical director's voice was iced with sarcasm, "kindly enlighten me with your evaluation, Doctor."

"I think there's a chance—very slight, I admit—if we operate soon enough. The kid's pulmonary pressure could blow within forty-eight hours. In my opinion, if we don't get in there by tomorrow, or the next day at latest, it *will* be too late. It's the child's last and only chance to live, slight as it is, and I think it's our duty as doctors to give her that chance."

Strang let out a short, bitter laugh. " 'Duty' is hardly a foreign word to me, Cane. May I remind you that I live under a crushing sense of duty twenty-four hours a day? Every day I am compelled to turn away operable as well as inoperable patients because we simply can't handle them all. It is my responsibility to admit only those, on a selective basis, who in my considered opinion can be most benefited."

"I am not questioning your selective judgment, sir, but—"

Strang waved him to silence. "Your concern for the patient is to be admired, but as an old pro with at least a twenty-five years' edge on your experience, let me give you a bit of advice. Too much concern is a serious handicap, and you must outgrow it. Most doctors start out having enormous empathy for patients and their families. In the beginning, they tend to get involved with all of them. But to work in the cardiovascular field you have to develop a shield around you. When someone dies, they die. You can't crack up. Caths go on, surgery goes on. There'll be a dozen new patients tomorrow."

"That may be true, sir, but in the case of this child, I ask that you reconsider your decision—if only as a special favor to me." Adam got the words out with difficulty. It was too uncomfortably close to begging, and a breach of his own ethics to ask for or give favored treatment.

Strang frowned. "I could not possibly accommodate your highly unusual request—even if I wanted to. Directly after the aneurysm operation tomorrow forenoon, I'm flying to Chicago to attend the annual meeting of the Midwest Heart Association, and shall have to stay overnight for special award ceremonies the following day. I have no choice but to attend—" he allowed himself a faint smile—"since I'm to be honored for my achievements in cardiovascular surgery. That puts me another day behind and only reinforces my answer to your request, which is a definite 'no'."

"Then I have only one last request to make—" Adam took a deep breath and continued, "Allow me to perform the operation."

"Surely you're joking, Cane!"

"It seems a reasonable enough request to me, sir. Naturally, I would expect to assume total responsibility so that if the operation failed, it would be no blemish on your reputation."

"*Your* responsibility!" The surgical director's face was stormy. "Are you not aware that I—and I alone—am directly responsible for everything that happens in the surgical division, including the welfare of patients assigned to you? Do you not realize the immense cost in time, money, personnel, and equipment involved in a single operation of the type you propose to attempt? And yet you have the gall, the effrontery, to ask permission to *practice* your puny skills in an effort to perform a high-risk operation that I've already advised you is hopeless? You expect me to condone such an unconscionable waste of valuable hospital resources on an operation surely doomed to failure when there are so many waiting in line who can be helped? Cane, you are an utter fool!"

Adam waited a few high-tension moments of silence, trying to ignore the stinging rise of anger. "If I'm such a fool and my skills are so puny," he said stiffly, "why was I appointed surgical fellow and your assistant?"

"Even I can make mistakes, Cane. At one time I thought you showed great promise. I had hopes that you would develop along the lines I had envisioned for you. To that end, I gave unstintingly of my time to train you, I assigned patients on whom you could practice within the limits of your medical abilities, and exercised the greatest patience when your efforts fell so far short of expectations. But my patience is giving out. Unless I see a sudden and dramatic improvement in both your attitude and medical performance, I shall feel obliged to withdraw my endorsement of you as a suitable candidate for the field of cardiovascular surgery."

"Am I to take that as a threat to my career?"

"You are free to interpret it as you like."

"The only possible interpretation is that I've become the victim of your personal spite, sir. I have no apologies to make for either my attitude or work performance. I happen to be a goddamned hard worker and a Grade A-1 surgeon—and you know it. So what are your *real* motivations for holding me in check— limiting me to surgical procedures far below my capabilities?" Adam had grown pale and tense with long-repressed anger, and even knowing he was cutting his own throat with his own tongue, plunged on. "Can it be that you suffer from irrational fears that my skills, if given a fuller range, might overtake yours?"

"Aren't you acting a bit paranoid, Cane?" Strang's face had turned pink but his tone was deceptively mild.

"My intention is only to clarify the situation, sir."

Strang smiled thinly. "If you haven't grasped it yet, I'll spell it out. You are—in effect—my employee, and I am empowered at any time—by the mere formality of so recommending to the hospital board—to effect your dismissal. More important, for the three years you have trained with me, I have been the sole judge and repository of your medical performance records, which are in my files. Should you continue to disappoint me, or attempt anything so rash as taking any of your imaginary grievances over my head to the hospital board— of which I also happen to be a member—I would make certain that you never again hold a responsible position in hospital medicine anywhere in this country. Is that clear enough?"

"Very clear, sir—" Adam paused, looking at the floor—"and I offer you my deepest apology."

The surgical director visibly relaxed. A slight smile touched his lips. "Perhaps there's hope for you yet, Cane," he said with a tinge of warmth. "I'm a reasonable man, and I think you'll find me quite able to overlook, to a certain extent, words spoken in haste and regretted later—providing I am convinced that you are ready to develop a more cooperative attitude. The important thing is to know when your medical judgment is in error, and not repeat the same mistake twice."

"I wasn't apologizing for my medical judgment, sir."

"Then for what?"

"I apologize for my failure to understand you—as I do now."

Strang's trace of a smile grew tolerant. "And what is it that you understand about me now that you didn't before?"

"What I understand about you now, sir, is that you're a totally coldblooded, ruthless, surgical machine. I apologize for thinking you could be guilty of the human weakness of even one small spark of compassion for others."

Adam spun around and went out.

In her room in the Children's Pavilion, eleven year old Holly Robbins took a sip from a glass of orange juice the nurse had just brought and looked up questioningly. "Do you know yet how soon it will be before they operate on my sick heart, Miss Herbst?"

"That kind of information is generally not known by nurses in advance, dear. In due time, the doctors will tell you."

"Gee, I wish they'd hurry. I get scared every time my heart starts jumping around like crazy."

"Everybody's doing all they can. These things take a lot of time and preparation."

"I guess my case *is* kind of special." Holly smiled, a bit proudly. "Are there any other girls in the hospital with a bad heart like mine, waiting to get operated on?"

"None that I know of."

"Do you know anyone who did get an operation like mine?"

"At the moment I can't recall any that were *exactly* like yours."

"Do they always do a good job fixing up hearts?"

"Of course, of course. They'll fix you up fine."

"Gosh, it's going to be wonderful when I can run and play games like other kids, and then, when I get to high school, start dating and dancing with boys."

"Yes, you have a lot to look forward to." Nurse Herbst had finished bustling around and gathering up things in a tray, preparatory to leaving.

"Miss Herbst, could you stay awhile longer and play a game of S.O.B. with me? That's a card game, you know, and if you haven't played it, I could teach you."

"I'd love to, dear, but I'm afraid I have just too many chores left to do."

"How come some patients, like I see on some television programs, get to have a nurse all the time and here I am alone so much?"

"Well, those are special duty nurses. They work with very, very sick patients or people who need very special attention. And they are very expensive because there aren't enough to go around.

"Oh, I see . . ." When the problem was put in terms of expense, Holly understood clearly, because it was the kind of problem she'd often overheard discussed by her parents in solemn, resigned voices.

"I've got to rush now, dear. Bye, bye."

"Goodbye, Miss Herbst." Glumly, Holly sipped at her orange juice and decided she'd play another game of solitaire.

On the bulletin board, the names of the interns were listed under one of the four hospital services (Medicine, Surgery, Obstetrics, and Pediatrics) to which they had been assigned, along with the names of the resident doctor to whom they would report.

Steve Wolosyk found his name under Surgery, and the supervising doctor was Dr. Adam Cane, Assistant Chief of the Surgical Division. Not bad for a starter! Actually, Steve had little interest in surgery—his ambition was to become a specialist in internal medicine— but that morning he'd heard from one of the outgoing interns (now a full-fledged doctor) that Cane was one of the best—a tough but nice guy to work for.

His glance flicked to the other lists and skimmed over the names until he found it—*Wheeler, Donna.* Under Medicine I. He turned. She was still looking at the bulletin board. He sensed that she sensed he was looking at her, and to break the constraint, said, "What service did you get?"

"Medicine I."

"I got Surgery."

"So I noticed."

He felt a definite jump in his heartbeat. Was that a sign, her checking out his assignment on the list?

"What do you plan to go into eventually?" he said.

She turned and looked at him and he saw no sign at all. Her face was a polished mask of disinterest. An odd thing about her color was that he had always been vaguely repelled by black skin to a degree increasing with its darkness, but on her now . . . it wasn't as if he'd been suddenly struck blind to it, but more as if something in him had snapped, or done a flip-flop, and he wanted to touch her, stroke her, feel the silky-smooth texture of her skin, almost *because* she was black.

"Pediatrics," she said. "I like working with children."

"You ought to be good at it. I mean, women—"

"I know. Women are queasy about blood and all that garbage, and if they must elbow their way into doctoring, let them stick to the soft, mothery kind that comes natural—but you got it backwards, Wolosyk. I could slice open a white belly without batting an eyelash, only it just happens I think I can do more good for the kids."

"That's not how I meant it."

"No matter." She glanced at her wristwatch. "If you'll excuse me, I'm going to scoot off and look up my new lord and master, Dr. Langsteen. I'm told he's a slavedriver who unloads about thirty unsuspecting patients on every new intern assigned to him, and I can hardly wait to start stuffing pills into all those shocked faces."

She started away, the supple body all easy grace, a subtle little swing twitching the white cloth of skirt against her buttocks, the muscles of her dark legs pulling and tightening with each step.

"Oh—Miss Wheeler," he called. "I mean, *Doctor . . .*"

She turned and gave him a quick glance, clearly puzzled, but with a slight questioning smile. This time he thought he saw in her eyes a sign and was emboldened.

"Yes?"

"I was just thinking that since we're both new here, you might like to go out with me tomorrow evening. I've got a little sleep to catch up on first, and . . ."

Her smile faded. "Look, Wolosyk, let's get one thing straight right from the start. I'm not what you're hoping for. You want an easy little black lay to jolly up your boring days here at the hospital. Well, I just don't have any jollies to give you, Doctor, and if I did, the last guy in the world I'd ever let touch my little old black ass would be a big white Polack from Hamtramck. Why don't you just go try somewhere else? I hear tell there's good hunting among the white nurses."

Steve flushed, a little from anger but also from embarrassment. She had unerringly picked up on the lust that had seized him, but he hadn't expected a rebuff. Not from a black girl. From childhood days he had grown up absorbing like a sponge all the attitudes and conditionings reflected by the males around him toward the neighboring black community—one of the more pervasive beliefs being that black women were innately sex-oriented, more eager for it as well as immeasurably more talented at it than any white girl could ever hope to be.

Goddamn hotpants Polack, he swore at himself, you've blown it.

"You've got me wrong," he said.

"Maybe, but just maybe ..." He liked the hard scorn in her eyes as they slashed at him. "I can read that big, square-jawed, all-Americanized face of yours like an open book, Wolosyk—only I'm another kind of book you're just judging by the color of its cover."

"So what the Christ is wrong with it if I am turned on by you?" Steve said, thoroughly angry now. "I'm not the only guy—white *or* black—who's going to get charged up by you, and if that's hard for you to accept, you better see a shrink. I didn't ask you to tumble in bed with me, for God's sake. I only asked you to go out with me."

She smiled, slightly. "Like where did you have in mind? Orchestra seats to the Detroit Philharmonic—or a back-door tour into your bachelor quarters?"

Steve hadn't really thought much about it until now. He had hazily thought of perhaps taking her to dinner in some dim-lighted, out-of-the-way place, with drinks, and afterwards—who knew what? But then there was that informal bash he'd heard about from one of the other interns that morning—the idea had bored him, but under the circumstances . . .

"I heard that one of last year's interns, who's staying on as a resident, is having an open house party to celebrate, and all new interns are invited. The word is supposed to get passed around that anyone bringing their own bottle is welcome. I thought we could have dinner first, and then—"

"I'll tell you what, Wolosyk. We'll give it a try. Just this once."

eight

The man in the gray suit was about five-nine in height, almost slim, and had a hard clean face and the kind of grayish-blue cold eyes that looked born to win contests.

"Sit down, Mr. Tunstra," he said, indicating a chair.

"Would you mind telling me what this is all about?" said Mike, ignoring the chair and frowning at a uniformed officer seated near the desk. Only a few minutes ago, the administrator's secretary had called the orderly and, with no explanation, relayed an order for him to report to the small consultation room next to Personnel.

"My name's London." The voice was cool and crisp with a sense of its authority. "Sergeant Borman you've already met. We're here to ask a few questions, and the administrator has generously loaned us this room so that our interrogations won't upset hospital routine."

"But I've already told the sergeant everything I know," Mike said sullenly.

The paunchy sergeant, a loose-skinned, sallow man,

let his heavy lips twitch into a faint grin, which didn't at all change the shrewd cold look in his eyes.

"Just for the records," he said mildly, "tell Detective London the same story you told me the other night."

"The whole damn routine again?"

"Yeah—only this time fill in the blank spaces."

Resentfully, Mike recounted as briefly as possible his version of the wounded black man's arrival, the black girl's vanishing act, and how he'd parked the Stingray in accordance with administrative rules, after which he'd hustled back to EW.

The corners of the sergeant's lips twitched again. "It's still full of blank spaces, Tunstra. Think a little harder and tell us everything you can remember about the suitcase."

"Say, what the crap's coming off here?" said Mike in a forced outburst of anger. "I told you last night and I tell you again now—I didn't see any suitcase! Are you accusing me of lying?"

"Cool it, Mr. Tunstra," said London.

"Well, I don't like being accused and pestered like this. Before you waste any more time with stupid questions, I've got a citizen's right to know what it's all about."

"The suitcase we're looking for," said London, "contains ten to twelve kilos of pure heroin—that's two to three million dollars' worth, street value."

Mike felt a tingle of excitement—almost erotic—race up his spine. Almost three million stashed away down in his locker! He could feel a vein pulsing frenetically in his neck.

"And that's just a fraction of a shipment that's already been sold and divided among a dozen or more of the midwest contractors we're trying to track down before it gets to the wholesalers, who cut it and package it and continue the downward distribution until it reaches the pushers on the street. Thousands of them. The shipments keep coming and the distribution keeps spreading. Unless we can make in-roads into breaking-up the operation. But to do it, we need citizen cooperation." The detective leaned closer, his eyes bright and earnest. "Does that answer your citizen's concern, Mr. Tunstra? Do you understand now why we have to ask all these questions?"

"Uh, sure," said Mike uncomfortably, "only you're barking up the wrong tree picking on me." He knew they could prove nothing. The only two who could possibly know the suitcase had been in the Stingray were Speed Wilson—still in coma up in ICU, on the verge of death—and the black chick, who from the way she'd flaked off was probably back in Alabama by now. "If there was a suitcase in the car, like you say, the guys who shot up that black boy probably got it."

"The ones who shot Wilson are under arrest, Mr. Tunstra. As for the suitcase, it had been under constant police surveillance—intended as bait for an important connection in the interstate drug traffic. The attack on Wilson by other criminals was not anticipated, however. When Wilson's girl friend took over the driving and managed to escape their attackers, the suitcase was in the Stingray. We're certain it was still in the car when she reached the hospital."

Mike felt a trickle of moisture down his back and his palms were damp. "The girl could have tossed it out the window."

"Virtually impossible. The recorded timing shows that she had to be driving over ninety all the way to the hospital. The suitcase was heavy. Besides, an intensive search of the highway shoulders has been made, with negative results."

"She could have lugged it with her when she beat it the hell out of here."

"Let's stop all this bullshitting, Tunstra," said Borman. "The broad parked less than fifty feet from the

Emergency Ward entrance under floodlights bright as high noon. Dr. Holland, who was on duty with you, saw her clear enough to describe her and testify that to his knowledge she wasn't carrying a thing. You were the first one out there with the stretcher—at least ten feet ahead of Dr. Holland—so that already makes you a liar when you claim you couldn't get a close look at her."

"Like I tried to tell you last night," Mike said hotly, "I was more concerned with helping the poor bastard all shot up than ogling some chick's legs. Why don't you find her and ask her about it instead of—"

The phone on the desk rang shrilly, and London picked it up. After a brief, monosyllabic interchange with the caller, he hung up and looked at Borman. "The report on the Stingray just came in. It's a roller."

Mike felt relief. A 'roller', he knew, was a stolen car often used by criminals to screw up police efforts in tracing them. They'd never find the black girl now!

Borman shrugged. "I could have told you. One of the ways you can always spot these Jones guys, they like to drive gold-plated El Dorados." He shifted his attention back to Mike. "As I was saying, Tunstra, let's cut the horseshit."

"Excuse me, Sergeant," said Mike with a snotty grin. "I quite clearly recall that awhile ago, your reference was to 'bullshit'."

"Let's settle for cowshit," said Borman imperturbably. "What it boils down to, you were the only one who had a chance to get at that suitcase. Now if you've got enough smarts to cover a pinhead, you'll tell us what you did with it before you get some of that cowshit shoved back down your throat."

"I've got enough smarts to know that after I parked the 'ray, anybody could have come along and ripped off anything that was in it. Couldn't you figure that out for yourself, Sergeant?"

Borman's heavy lips pulled tight into a half grin, half

snarl. "I deal in facts. First important fact is that only the police and the Mafia knew about that suitcase. The police don't have it, and the Mafia don't either. Two carloads of Bonaro's shitheelers have been out there cruising around since last night. Like bees after honey. Know who Bonaro is?"

"Sure, I hear he's the new presidential advisor," said Mike, straining to be flip but feeling a sudden, clutching sensation in his guts. Anyone who read the Detroit papers knew about Bonaro. A Mafia sub-chief. Routinely he was hauled into court on charges involving the numbers racket, drugs, extortion, prostitution, murder, every criminal activity in the book, and always walked out again a free man—one of those increasingly common cases where everybody "knows" the facts but the courts couldn't, or wouldn't, prove them. To Mike, Bonaro was a savage force far more to be feared than the police.

"Too bad he ain't your advisor. He could tell you there ain't a chance in the world of getting that suitcase out of here. The entire hospital premises are fenced in, only one road out, and that's plugged airtight. Every hear of dope-sniffing dogs, Tunstra? We got two of the best in the country flown in last night. Special trained for heroin. You could seal just one grain in plastic or metal and those dogs could pick it up twenty feet away. One sniff of it, they go crazy."

"Say, why the Christ are you feeding me all this crap? I could make a lot of trouble for you guys, accusing me like this."

Borman looked expressionlessly at the detective. "I didn't hear that, Jerry, did you?"

Plainly, London didn't approve of Borman's approach. "We're not accusing you, Mr. Tunstra. We're merely seeking information. Sergeant Borman inadvertently misstated himself.

"All right," said Borman. "I backtrack. You're not being accused—not yet. Just warned."

"One more thing," said London. "Within the next twenty-four hours—as soon as administrative red tape has been cleared—we're beginning a complete hospital search—"

"That means a real army shakedown, Tunstra. Inch by inch."

London frowned at Borman's interruption, and continued, "We're only telling you this in hopes that if you should obtain—or recall—any information pertaining to the suitcase, you'll realize how extremely important it is to notify police officials immediately. Any information leading to the prompt recovery of the suitcase, anything that could save us the considerable trouble and enormous expense of an intensive search, would of course be properly appreciated." He smiled at Mike and gave a nod of dismissal. "Thank you, Mr. Tunstra."

"And for what it's worth," added Borman, "here's my last warning. I haven't got all the facts—yet—but I got a damn good supply of what you might call 'cop intuition'. I can promise I'm going to find that junk, and when I do, I personally guarantee that somebody's ass is going to fry—and you can bet your skinny little ass on that."

Nurse Kerri Kozak was exhausted. The day had been long, the work hard and continuous, but the drain on her energies had been more emotional than physical. One of the more saddening duties had been to prep another corpse for the morgue—this time, the sweet-faced boy of eighteen who had died that forenoon of a brain hemorrhage caused by a motorbike accident. Equally heartbreaking had been the sense of futility in attending Natalie Tyler who though she knew she was dying of cancer was making superhuman efforts to conceal the ever-increasing pain despite top allowable dosages of Demerol, the synthetic morphine pain-killer.

Approaching Natalie's room now, Kerri took comfort in the knowledge that in about ten more minutes she would go off duty and a nurse on the evening shift— hopefully more inured to suffering—would take over. Meanwhile, she had this last visit to make. Natalie had asked for letter writing materials, which Kerri was delivering.

Just outside the door she hesitated at the sound of voices inside raised in apparent argument—Natalie shrill and demanding, her husband Dave remonstrating. Discreetly knocking, Kerri waited a few moments and entered.

Seeing Kerri, Natalie smiled. "Ah, deliverance! Kerri, as a dear friend of mine, I want to enlist your help in persuading this dunderhead of a husband that he's simply *got* to get air reservations and fly out to California tonight or tomorrow—as soon as possible."

"I'm afraid I'm neither trained nor qualified to help in a family argument," said Kerri, placing the writing materials on a bedside stand.

"I'd say you're ideally qualified—you're blessed with kindness and good sense, so—"

"Natalie," said Dave, "can't you see you're only creating more embarrassment by trying to get Kerri involved?"

"Who gives a damn about embarrassment? That's trivia. What I'm trying to tell you is *important*. Kerri—"

"Natalie, *please*—cut it off!"

"Like hell I will. Kerri, you're *our* friend—Dave's as well as mine—so I want you to know what it's all about. Poor Dave, who happens to be one of the best aerospace engineers in the country, got knocked out of his job a couple months ago because of government cutbacks in the space program—at a time when we were already broke because of my goddamn medical bills, and borrowing right and left just to keep going. Did you know our medical insurance doesn't pay out-patient medical expenses? You've got to be *in* some lousy hospital just to collect *part* of what it costs. Anyway, it seems that now things are picking up a little, and a couple days ago Dave got a good job offer from a missile plant out in California—but what does he do? Race out there and grab it? No! He's just sitting around here on his can!"

"Natalie," said Dave with strained patience, "it's just a waste of time to argue, and I'm sure that Kerri understands why I couldn't possible leave at a time like this."

"But it could be weeks, *months* before I die."

"Natalie, *please* . . ." Dave caught one of her hands and clasped it tight. His eyes blurred.

"Now both of you listen to me—Dave and you, too, Kerri. Let's be realistic. I'm no longer the number one consideration around here. I've written myself off, and let's face it, so have you—so we can stop playing hypocritical little games. Dave, darling, from now on it's not my life that counts—it's only yours that's important—and whatever little time I have left will be a lot happier if I know that you're going to be all right."

Dave's eyes were streaming tears. "Darling—" his voice choked.

"You see what I'm trying to do, Kerri? I'm trying to get this sentimental oaf to let me die in peace and the happiness of knowing he's snagged that all-important job—but if he doesn't get out there fast, I can assure you there are umpty-ump other qualified engineers ready to grab it. These days, they aren't going to hold that kind of job for him. It's not just the money—although God only knows I've bled him dry. If Dave doesn't have a job to stabilize him when—when the time comes, he'll fall apart. I know this darling man of mine only too well."

Dave had bent forward, face bowed against the flatness that had once been Natalie's breasts, his shoulders quivering. Natalie stroked his hair.

"I'll have to leave now," Kerri said uncomfortably, "but if there's anything else you need . . ."

"There's one last favor I'd like to ask, Kerri."

"I'll do anything I can."

"Dave hasn't been getting enough sleep, and that's one reason his judgment isn't up to par right now— how long can you go on just brooding every night and trying to knock yourself out with a jug of Scotch? Please use your influence around this place to get Dave some sleeping pills. With a good, long rest, I know he'll look at things more objectively and I'll be able to make him see what is really best in the long run."

"I'm sure any of the doctors will give him a prescription that he can get filled anywhere."

"But I want to *know* that he's got them, Kerri. Dave's so absent-minded. In his present state, he's sure to misplace a prescription or forget to fill it. So be a sweetheart, Kerri, and get the prescription and have it filled in the hospital pharmacy and then come back and tuck it away in Dave's pocket so I can be *sure* he'll go home and get a good sleep."

"I'll see what I can do," said Kerri, and went out.

The first doctor she encountered in the corridor was the neurosurgeon, Mel Kloster. Briefly, she told him of Natalie's request.

"I wish it was always this easy," he said, taking out his prescription book. "That poor bastard is in for a lot of miserable nights before it's all over—so I'd better make it a full month's supply."

nine

Seated at his desk, Victor Strang stared moodily at his hands. In the gathering dusk of early evening—he had purposely not turned on any of the office lights—the pale, slender fingers had the look of graceful little puppet figures dancing in a row as he continued for a few minutes his daily routine of flexing, contracting, bending, until all the small muscles of the hands had been fully exercised. They were beautiful hands—strong, supple, endowed with a deftness and cunning all their own—yet hands that had betrayed him.

No longer could he blind himself to the terrible truth. The spasticity, the ataxia, the growing stiffness were unmistakable. His surgeon's dexterity was vanishing.

During the several operations he'd performed today, he again had fumbled a couple times. Nothing serious. The patients would make a fine recovery and never know the difference. Nor had any of the operating team noticed—except Cane. Damn the man!

Actually, he'd known but refused to face it even before last night—which is one reason he'd erupted with
such anger at Cane then, and again this forenoon when
Cane had dared to point the finger of blame. In the
secret depth of his soul, Strang knew his anger for what
it really was—the hot defensiveness of guilt. For guilty
he was. Karl Lentz was the very dead proof of it. Proof
that would soon be buried. By long distance telephone
call to Lentz' only relative, a sister, he had arranged
for shipment of the body and by artful, condoling
words extracted from her the admission that she didn't
like the idea of an autopsy. He assured her that her
wishes would be respected. Nobody would ever know
for sure whether Lentz' death during the night had
been due to the inability of his weakened body to with-
stand the massive surgical assault, or because the surgery itself was faulty. Not even Cane.

Strang alone knew, and this knowledge, along with
other unbearable thoughts, would soon settle like
murky sediment to the secret depth of his soul where
he never had to look at them again.

Not so the hands that had failed him. He looked at
them with loathing. What was it? As a doctor and the
disciplined custodian of his own body, he should
quickly be able to diagnose the causes, but the onset of
symptoms had been so gradual, so insidious, and the
demands of his cardiovascular world had left little time
to delve more than superficially into the other specialized worlds of diseases of the musculoskeletal system,
the joint disorders, and the still largely unsolved mys-
teries of the arthritides.

Slowly, he began massaging the fingers of one hand,
feeling carefully for slight swellings, tenderness, the tiny
nodes of degenerative joint disease that followed destruction of hyaline cartilage. There was nothing. No
swelling, no osteophytic overgrowth, no pain.

Clinging to that tiniest of clues—no pain—his brain

raced, sorting through diagnostic experience, flipping the card files of memory. Was it synovial—a defect of the synovial membranes causing insufficiency of the lubricating fluids they secreted between the finger joints? Muscular atrophy? Some circulatory or central nervous system involvement? Or—

It came to him suddenly like a small light bursting from innumerable bits of forgotten notes, ignited by the true physician's greatest asset—medical intuition.

Picking up a letter opener, he jabbed the sharp point viciously into several of his fingers, tearing the skin of one and bringing a speck of blood. But feeling no pain. Dropping the opener, he reached for the silver cigarette lighter kept for visitors—Strang didn't smoke—and struck a light. Holding it close beneath an extended forefinger, he watched the lambent flame curl around his flesh. Still no pain, no sense of heat. Bending, he scrubbed a hand over the thick-napped rug. The sensitivity of his touch against the nubby texture was so acute that he even felt a few grains of sand imbedded in the wool.

The *feeling* was there. Feeling without pain.

Syringomyelia! Of course.

Of unknown causes, syringomyelia was a disease of the spinal cord and medulla, a progressive, sneaky disease that could remain underground, undetected for years while slowly attacking the gray matter of the cord—eventually destroying the fibers of pain and temperature as they crossed a juncture of the spinal cord on their way to the brain. The earliest symptom was dissociated sensory loss—loss of pain and temperature sense, with retention of touch, soon followed by atrophy and weakness of the hand muscles and loss of muscular coordination.

Prognosis unpredictable. It could go fast, it could inch along so slowly as to seem stationary for many years, but the disease process never stopped. It would spread next to the shoulders, face, lower extremities. More serious effects would follow—cavitation, gliosis, nystagmus, scoliosis. Ultimately, paralysis, aspiration pneumonia—and death.

There was no cure.

Strang felt a sheen of dampness on his forehead, a vague unease in his chest. Automatically he reached for a wrist and checked his pulse, finding it of clinical interest that his mental disturbance alone—despite his doctor's detachment—could so quickly accelerate his heartbeat, increase the pulmonary pressures.

From an inner jacket pocket he took two small unlabeled bottles, shook out a tablet from each, swallowing one with a glass of water from a decanter on the desk. The swallowed tablet was digitalis. It would slow the overworking heart ventricles and relieve pressure in the lung vessels. The other tablet, which was nitroglycerine, he slipped under his tongue where it would dissolve and relieve the mild chest distress.

That Victor Strang had been for most of his adult life a victim of congestive left heart failure—a result of rheumatic fever that left him with a damaged aortic valve—was a secret unknown by any of his hospital associates, not even by his wife. He had hidden it well and learned to live with it by pacing his efforts and skilled management of his body. Far from bemoaning his weakened heart, he viewed it as the foundation of his character. It had forced him into austere living habits, taught him not to waste energies, developed his strength of will. By exercising care, he was able to lead a reasonably active life, and expected it to be a long one.

That is, such had been his expectations up until now.

How much longer did he have? One year? Five years? Longer? Some cases had been known to survive up to forty years after onset—but as invalids, bodies near useless.

Hands incapacitated.

How much longer did he dare perform surgery? Was the time left for the diminishing skills in his fingers to be measured in hours? Days? Weeks? Or with luck—

The phone shrilled and he at once picked up the receiver. Even seconds were not to be wasted.

It was his wife, Leslie.

"Vic, I'm glad I got you before you left. I just thought you ought to know that I won't be coming home tonight."

"Thank you for being so kind as to inform me."

"It's the least I can do . . ." Her cool voice, with still the snobbish, Eastern accent acquired at Vassar, softened a bit. "And Vic, about last night—"

"I prefer not to discuss it, Leslie," he said tersely.

"All I wanted to say is I'm truly sorry—" there was a tinge of sadness in her voice, "although it had to happen . . ."

"I already consider it past history," he said, and hung up.

Her call had deepened his depression, and making an effort to shunt the problem of Leslie from his thoughts, he got up and went to the window. The sun had vanished below the horizon but still ignited the bellies of a few southwestern clouds above a long, low auto plant in the distance.

It was all too symbolical, he thought. The sense of being in his sunset, prematurely—soon to be declining into obscurity with only a few pale reflections of his former brilliance.

Why had it struck him? Strang believed not at all in predestined fate, but totally in cause and effect. The secret of the syringomyelia was locked somewhere within his bodily mechanisms—perhaps an inborn error of metabolism—but there to be found. And if found, perhaps eradicated.

One of his beliefs was that disease could only take

hold when predisposing factors were present such as fatigue, malnutrition, inborn defects, or insufficient cardiac output. One of his deepest, almost mystic convictions was that the heart was the root of nearly all bodily evils. Most ailments from skin rashes to ulcers were traceable by a complex series of interlinking and crosslinking chains through the tissues, glands, nerves, body fluids, organs, and other components back to a starting point located somewhere in the heart or its circulatory system. Many so-called "primary" diseases were actually secondary disorders resulting from more basic flaws and diseases of the cardiovascular structure. When healthy young volunteer prisoners, for example, were injected with deadly viruses, their natural immunological defenses—nourished and maintained in tiptop shape by superb young hearts and arteries—most of them were able to throw off the disease with ease.

Everything depended on the heart. With an invincible mechanical heart transistorized for eternity and replaceable sets of Dacron arteries and veins with Teflon valves, he thought wryly, one could theoretically live forever.

A vulgar thought intruded—and be a perfect lover. Imagine copulating for eternity! He grimaced with distaste.

That had been Leslie's hang-up. Raw sex. Unfortunately, he had not known it at the time he married her right after her graduation from Vassar. She was twenty-two then and he thirty-seven—a fifteen year age gap—but that was not the problem. The problem was biological and temperamental. Not being a sensual man, he had put his emphasis on tender closeness, mature communication, and expectations that she would enjoy the privilege of being the perfect doctor's wife—a gay, charming hostess, socially correct in all ways, and happily subservient to all his needs. Their sex life was scanty, and dreaded because he paid so heavily—an abrupt drop in his energies for days afterwards.

Although Leslie didn't complain as their sexual encounters became more and more infrequent—his unspoken excuse being that increasing responsibilities at the hospital so exhausted him at the end of days sometimes stretching to eighteen hours at a time that he wanted only to relax briefly with a brandy before sleep—her growing, sullen restiveness spoke for itself. Fortunately, she had a cultured taste in the arts and spent much of her time going to symphonies, opera, the art galleries, and other such activities. It had pleased him to believe that she fully sublimated her unused sexual energies in this way and didn't suffer in the least from their lack of physical intimacy.

Until last night. Lately it had been shock after shock, so to speak.

When he had gone home at ten last night—shaken by the by-pass on Lentz and Adam's outrageous insurgence—Leslie was not there. Which was not unusual. Often she didn't get home until after he was asleep. His usual evening routine was to browse through medical journals while sipping his allotted two ounces of brandy before retiring at eleven. By eleven, Leslie still hadn't returned. Breaking precedent, he indulged in another brandy, for the tranquilizing effects, and decided to wait up for her. He was depressed and mildly furious about Adam and Ilse, and felt a strong need to talk, to feel a bit of closeness, warmth.

Waiting, he brooded about the falling out with Ilse. She had long supplied the warmth, the understanding that Leslie lacked, but after today . . . It started a slight trembling in his arms and hands just to remember that Ilse had dared to suggest that he lean more heavily on Adam to carry his operational load, had the temerity to say that Adam could quite capably handle any of the difficult major cases. For such brash, surgical ignorance he could have forgiven her, but not for that other thing—her cheap, primal attraction to Cane.

Strang boiled at the thought. In preference to *him*.

It was long after one before Leslie got home. Unsteady on her feet.

"Oh—you're still up, Vic?" she said in a slurred voice.

"An acute observation," he said coldly. He'd never before seen her intoxicated and was both shocked and enraged. "May I ask the meaning of this?"

"Of what?" she said with a feigned expression of innocence.

"Staggering home like a drunken tramp."

She frowned down at her legs—hidden beneath a long dress of satiny pale yellow—as if they were guilty partners in sin who had somehow betrayed her. "I wasn't aware that I was staggering."

"Stop quibbling, Leslie. I demand that you explain yourself."

Sliding off her Italian knit shawl, she tossed it over a chair, baring shapely shoulders that were deeply tanned from lounging in a bikini every afternoon beside the pool. At forty-four, double the age when he'd married her, Leslie was still a stunning female. Her waist was still flat, her nice figure only slightly heavier, and the silken, blonde hair was, if anything, even more exotic (thanks to one of the exclusive Detroit beauty temples, from which he got outrageous monthly bills). Most of her changes, he thought, were of the hidden kind but reflected in an intangibly coarser expression of the eyes and mouth.

"Do you really want to know, Vic?"

"I thought I expressed myself very explicitly."

"Then I'll be just as explicit. I was out getting fucked."

He felt the heat rising slowly to his face, and then the sudden pulsing of his carotid artery, and knew that despite her words—the most shocking and in their full import most insulting words ever uttered to him—he had to force himself into calmness.

"Would you elaborate on that, please?"

"You want the graphic details?"

With immense effort, he kept his voice steady. "Just explain to me, if you can—why?"

She ran a hand through her silken coiffeur. "I like it. In fact, I'm crazy for it. Maybe I'm basically a nympho. That's not your fault and I don't think it's mine—but under the circumstances—not getting any of it at home—how long did you think I could go on being the pure, faithful wife?"

"How long did you?"

"A lot longer than I should have—" her voice had taken on a bitter, nasty edge, "in fact, it wasn't until a few years ago that I couldn't any longer take being the wife of an impotent husband, and went out looking."

A dizziness rose to his head and he walked over to the little bar next to the liquor cabinet and poured another brandy.

"I think I'll join you," she said.

"Brandy?"

"If you please."

He returned with the filled glasses and kept his hand steady as he handed it to her.

"That was a low blow," he said.

"Maybe I was wrong. Maybe you've been saving it all up to give to that little playmate of yours—what's her name? Ilse whosis or something."

He flushed again. "Ilse has been a dear friend. Nothing more."

She looked steadily into his eyes, probing. "I believe you, Vic. You've been secretive, but I grant you this. You've never lied to me."

He became reflective and stared into his glass. "Tell

me, Leslie, if I've been so—inadequate for your needs as a husband, why didn't you ask for a divorce?"

"I waited too long, and now there's no need. I'm happy enough with the present situation."

His eyes narrowed. "You mean you intend to go on with this outside thing?"

"Why not?"

"What if I divorced you?"

She smiled at him mockingly, her face chiseled and hard. "You won't. You've been ingrained from childhood with the hypocritical attitudes of the stodgy old pseudo-blue-blooded family you came from. For people of your ilk, divorce for any reason is a scandal, and when it brings out publicly sexual matters of an embarrassing nature, it's worse than murder."

"Do you not consider it hypocritical of yourself to pretend to be a faithful, devoted wife, when the opposite appears to be true?"

"You didn't marry me to be a bed partner, Vic. All you wanted was a socially proper wife to trot out on suitable occasions—and I've been that, have I not?"

"I expected more. What if our friends and social acquaintances ever found out about your infidelity?"

"Screw your friends and social acquaintances!"

"Is that vulgarity part of what you learned at Vassar or something you've picked up from more recent experience?"

"I learned that and plenty more at Vassar—including your cherished value of discretion. I've taken great care to protect your pride and reputation by being, let us say, very *underground* about my little affairs. But I can hardly call it discretion on your part when the whole hospital knows of your involvement with a sexy-looking nurse—although frankly, I'd like to believe it's not all so innocent as you say, because otherwise the poor girl's getting cheated."

Turning to conceal his stinging humiliation, he said

with forced casualness, "You just used the plural, 'affairs'. Am I to understand you have—or had—more than one lover?"

"If you really must know, there've been quite a few."

He battled against the compulsion to go on, and lost. "Do I know any of them?"

"One or two." Her smile was deliberately provoking.

He wanted to chop it off before it was too late, but the curiosity was too great.

"Was Adam Cane one of them?"

Her smile turned bitchy cold and there was a flash of hatred in her eyes. "I haven't yet had the opportunity—but I'm working on it."

For the first time in his fifty-nine years, Victor Strang totally lost control of himself. With a hoarse cry, he flung his glass aside and leaped toward her. Startled, she backed away, but he followed and grabbed her by the throat, bearing her back against a wall, where he started banging her head against the paneling. "I'll kill you!" he choked out.

At first she was terrified and fought with her fingers to tear his hands away, but as soon as she realized she could still breathe, she let herself go limp and looked up at him with sly eyes and a mocking smile.

"Go ahead and kill me if you want to," she said, "but what are you going to tell all your friends and social acquaintances tomorrow?"

He had a brief vision of familiar faces . . . shocked, condemning . . . but overriding it all was a sudden tiredness that made his arms turn heavy. Both ached, the left more than the right, and there was a pressing warmth in his chest. He let his hands fall away and stepped back, taking a deep breath. The pressure persisted and he was aware of slight sweating.

"Vic—you're so pale—"

He gestured toward the bar. "Be so kind—a glass of water."

"She got the water while he fumbled in his jacket for the pills. Swallowing one, getting the nitro under his tongue, he started away. Leslie stayed beside him, holding his arm.

"What is it, Vic?"

"Please . . ." He shook her hand away. "It's just a touch of dizziness. Too much overwork. I'll be fine after a good night's sleep."

In his bedroom, he clenched his left fist until the veins in the wrist stood out and with his right thumb took a careful pulse reading. Strong and steady, but still it was there—the premature beat, a compensatory pause, then back to regular. Another dozen beats, again the skipped beat, but less palpable. The chest pressure seemed lessened.

He knew precisely what had happened. Second stage block, a delay between the beat of the atrium and that of the ventricle long enough—more than 0.2 seconds—to prevent the electrical impulses of the heart nerves from passing from the atrium to the ventricle at the proper interval of time. A mild attack—the kind many men have and mistake for a touch of indigestion. Not an infarct, but a stern warning. With a patient he would have taken no chances, would have ordered him to a hospital, into oxygen. For himself he would have to rely on hairline decisions. There were compelling considerations.

Nobody must know.

He went to bed with a sedative and slept well.

Now, staring out into the early twilight sky, his thoughts shifted from last night's upsets over Leslie and his heart trouble and he began to examine with clinical detachment the larger problem, which was of more immediate concern—the syringomyelia.

There had to be a cure, and it *had* to be found. Damage already done, of course, was irreversible but conceivably could be stopped. And the clue, he was convinced, was to be found somewhere within the coronary network. Sometimes, he recalled, the disease was associated with vascular lesions, sometimes a cardiac muscle involvement—surgical problems. Tomorrow in Chicago, he would confide in one of his colleagues, arrange for a complete diagnostic check in a distant city, and perhaps—

There was a timid rapping on the office door, a timid call:

"Dr. Strang?"

"What is it, Glenna?"

The door opened. Light streaked across the shadowed floor and Glenna Woods' trim figure stood silhouetted in the doorway. "I'm sorry to intrude, but I couldn't help wondering if everything is all right—I mean, not seeing any lights under your door . . ."

"I appreciate your concern, Glenna, but everything's fine. I'm just mentally laying out the little talk I have to give at the association meeting tomorrow, and I think much better in darkness." He gave her one of his rare smiles. "I'm surprised you're still here. Isn't this long after office hours?"

"I'm aware of how hard you've been driving yourself, Doctor, and when you work late like this, I feel I ought to stay late, too, in case you need me."

He was touched. "That's very considerate of you, Glenna, but it's really not necessary. I think you ought to go now so you won't have to risk the ire of some waiting boy friend." Then suddenly remembering that sometimes she'd dated Adam Cane, and that morning—following his intuition—he'd asked her to try to get a phone call through to Cane at a number he jotted down for her—Ilse Jensen's—he wished he could recall his words.

"There's no boy friend waiting," she said evenly. "Before I go, are you sure there's no typing you'd like done? I'm very willing to do anything I can to make things a little easier for you—anything at all . . ."

"Thank you again," he said gently and walking over, chastely kissed her on the cheek. "Perhaps I'll take you up on your offer some other time. But for now, good night, Glenna."

"Good night, Doctor." Her smile was radiant.

At least he still had that, he thought ruefully after she was gone. They were still drawn to him, wanting to protect him. Until sooner or later . . .

Leslie—Ilse—and now Glenna, if he allowed it. Women by their very nature were inextricably bound to the vague or blatant yearnings of sex and he was unavoidably cast into the role of a bastard whenever his need for them nourished false hopes.

Leslie didn't know the full truth, and Ilse could only have wondered why he had never made any attempt to change their relationship from the completely platonic. It had been unfair to her—especially the snickering rumors of immorality—but even that he had needed for his *amour propre,* so to speak; he had used her as a sexual ego crutch. Not unlike the warped symbiosis between a rich old man, sexually feeble, and a lush young female he marries but can never hope to satisfy.

Yes, he thought morosely, looking down at his crotch, it always traces back to the heart. Even that symbol of masculinity, the whole font of male power—the testes—a man's balls, are worthless without a full flow of lifeblood. Not Leslie or Ilse or anyone else would ever know that it wasn't innate physical coldness that kept him free of lust—but only the simple biological fact that the severely inadequate circulation in his testes had begun their slow atrophy even in youth, and for many years now he had been totally impotent.

ten

Adam drove slowly. The twilight was hot and humid, the air rich with fumes of octane, oil, and lacquer from the big auto body plant a half mile away. Ahead where the hospital exit road ended, the intersecting freeway was a shimmering furrow of lights slicing a horizontal line between poison-laden skies and the murky earth. The streaming cars, he thought, had the look of giant mechanical ants racing meaninglessly in opposite directions, geared high, in frenetic haste to get—where? Factory workers anxious to get home to a cold beer, a hot supper, their favorite tv program? Kids impatient to go, go, go, to make the scene, greedy for life's excitements before the growing ballast of family, age, and proliferating credit card debts forced them to the sidelines? Early evening traffic always seemed infected with sick exuberance, a hellbent wildness, the tensions of insanity.

Beside him, Ilse said, "We're being flagged down, Adam. Have you been committing any crimes lately?" Ahead on the hospital road was a uniformed officer with an arm raised, and behind him, three police cars with revolving blue beacons on top.

"I've been contemplating one." A couple hours ago, knowing they'd both be working late, Adam had asked Ilse to join him for dinner.

She looked at him naughtily. "Are you looking for a partner in crime, maybe?"

"I'd need more than one."

"Oh dear. What's the nature of this sin, uh—I mean crime you're contemplating?"

"I'll confess it all a bit later." He pulled over to the side of the road, and a trooper thrust a head close to the car window.

"We'll have to hold you up for a few moments, Doctor," he said courteously. "Are you or your passenger carrying any Demerol, morphine, heroin, or opium on your persons or anywhere in the car?"

Adam and Ilse answered in the negative.

"You will both please step out of the car."

They got out. Another officer brought up a large German Shepherd on a leash. The dog eagerly leaped into the car and in a way almost human, briefly sniffed around in the front and back of the car, then backed out to be led around the car slowly by the officer.

"I thought the opium derivatives were almost odorless," Adam said to the first trooper curiously. "Can that dog really pick up the scent?"

"Even the synthetic stuff. One doctor forgot he had a packet of Demerol in his briefcase and the dog nearly tore it open with his teeth before we got it away from him."

"What's it all about?"

"Sorry, Doctor. I'm not permitted to discuss it."

The officer with the dog came up. "You're free to go now."

Back in the car, driving again, Ilse said, "I can see that some doctors really keep themselves insulated from what's going on in the world. Don't you ever read the papers?"

"A dedicated doctor only has time for the comics. It's refreshing to know that Dagwood—who must be about ninety by now—can keep on eating ten pounds of sliced garbage night after night, year after year, without a heart attack. And Snoopy—by dog years, which average about seven to every human year—he's nearing two hundred, and still no signs of arteriosclerosis."

"Does the dedicated doctor recall crying in his martinis last night about being an unwilling partner in crime to a by-pass operation on a certain Karl Lentz?"

"I seem to recall the name. By the way, has a post been done on the body yet?"

"You really are out of touch. The body, minus the post, is being transported on wings of love—that is, in a comfy, twenty-five-dollars-an-hour private but licensed hearse in strict accordance with state laws doubtless enacted with the connivance of the funeral directors' lobby—to a sweet little country cemetery far, far away."

"Then I'll never be able to confirm what I'm so damn certain about—that it was tamponade." Tamponade meant bleeding around the heart following faulty heart surgery, causing a fatal drop in blood pressure that could only be corrected—with luck—by emergency surgery.

"Dry your tears, Doctor. What I was about to tell you is that Lentz was a former numbers boss, and since the new laws making gambling legal in the state, he was moving into the drug racket. The speculation is that a big shipment of heroin he had with him got stolen and is still somewhere in the hospital."

"Sounds crazy. I knew the guy was loaded—all the special attention he was getting, and so forth—but crook or not, that's not the point. A doctor has got to be accountable for his work." It was one of the ironies of life, he thought, that a Lentz could be instrumental

in causing wrecked lives and death among thousands
and still get the best medical attention, the finest hospital resources that money could buy, whereas the innocent child, Holly Robbins, was to be turned away.

"While we're still on the subject of crime," she said,
"are you ready to tell me what you have in mind?".

"After a drink or two."

About fifteen minutes later at a corner table in the pleasant, dim-lit atmosphere of a small roadside inn, Ilse
raised her martini.

"A toast for your thoughts."

"They'd only bore or depress you."

"Try me, Adam—what's bugging you?"

"I had another run-in with Vic—a real bad one this
time."

"My toast," she said, "is to the nicest, most dedicated doctor I know." She took a long swallow from
her glass.

"Vic?"

"You, of course. The only doctor who's ever dared
speak his mind to Vic."

"But I'm not dedicated. Didn't you know that's an
obsolete term? It's been replaced by something more
realistic, perhaps more selfish, but still the only way to
hack it in today's medical world. These days the only
thing that counts is pure *professionalism,* a worship for
technical perfection. To a surgeon, all that should really
matter is that draped body on the table, prepped and
bared for incision—just a problem, a job. Any satisfaction to be derived comes from the surgical skill em-
ployed, and the final judgment is based only on whether
the patient lives or dies—not as a human life, you understand, but as some abstract equation the surgeon has
tried to solve. The moment you start thinking of the patient as an *individual,* with a family, joys, hopes, and so

forth, you're no longer up to the top level standards of modern medicine."

"Thanks for the lecture, Doctor," she said dryly, "but you're weaseling out, and a hell of a poor liar to boot. That was Vic Strang kind of talk—not anything I want to hear from Adam Cane. Now tell me what you two hassled about."

"Do you know anything about the pediatric VSD case?"

"Holly Robbins? Of course. Half the nurses in the Children's Pavilion have begun praying for her and stealing time from other duties to give her a little extra attention when you high and mighty professionalism doctors aren't looking."

"Well, they're wasting their time. Vic vetoed an operation."

"Why, for heaven's sake?"

Adam briefly summarized the high operational risk objections. "Even Don Wolff thinks it's hopeless to try," he added.

Ilse took an angry sip from her glass. "Do you think it's hopeless?"

"Almost. But the kid got under my skin somehow— which shows how unprofessional I am. My contention is that she's a goner anyway without the operation—the prognosis is a week or ten days at the most—so if there's even a whisper of a chance for her, which I think there is, we ought to try."

"Now you're back to talking like Adam Cane. Forget that garbage about professionalism without compassion. Could any surgeon be more compassionate than Christiaan Barnard, for example, and he's one of the all-time greats."

"Compassion didn't make him great. Barnard just happened to have the skills and the audacity to be the first surgeon in the world to do a human heart transplant."

"You've got the skills and the audacity too, so why don't you—" She stopped abruptly and her sea-green eyes widened in sudden comprehension. "Oh, now I'm beginning to pick up on it! How dense can I get? You wanted to do the operation yourself, and Vic turned you down—and that's what the hassle was all about. Right?"

"Right."

A middleaged, motherly waitress maneuvered her frilly white apron close to the table. "You folks ready to order dinner yet?"

Ilse looked at her nearly empty glass. "I think I'll hold off on the food for awhile and have another drink first."

"Make that double," Adam told the waitress.

"Okie, dokie. Two more martoonies coming up." The waitress ambled away.

Adam took a swig of his martini. "Are you trying to get me drunk again?"

"Not *that* drunk. At the proper time, I'll see that you get some solid food under your belt, but at the moment there are a few things I feel I must say to you, and I thought the Dutch courage of another drink might help." She lifted her glass to her lips.

Adam grinned. "Is this a proposal or a proposition?"

"Take your pick, but let's not rush it."

"I can be patient—up to a point."

"Adam—about Victor Strang, I know you think he must be a merciless, coldhearted bastard, but he's really not. He's a very troubled man with a lot of unsolved personal problems. I can even see his side of things in not wanting to operate on the child."

"I realize," Adam said with sudden coolness, "that having the advantage of knowing him on a much more intimate basis, you're more qualified to judge some aspects of his character."

Her eyes flared. "You know all about my 'intimate'

relationship with Vic, don't you? Everybody in the hospital gossips and snickers about it."

Adam tilted his head in a tiny bow. "My apologies if I seemed to imply any criticism. Your relationship with Strang is none of my business or concern. However, are you equally understanding about his refusal to let me operate on the kid?"

"Yes. It's because he hates you so much."

"So what else is new?"

"Vic's had a few surgical failures lately, as you know, and until—or unless—he recovers his confidence, he's afraid to try anything as difficult as the VSD case—so if you should try the operation, and succeed—"

"I know, he'd hate me even more."

"But certainly you realize that Vic's hate for you is really hate for himself. Self-haters, especially paranoics, turn their hate inside-out and project it outwards at the ones they think have all the things they lack."

Adam laughed. "What could the high and mighty Strang possibly think I have that he lacks?"

"Youth, health—and probably more surgical skill than he has—"

"I'll never buy that."

"It's his secret fear, nevertheless."

"A surgeon of his caliber should be far above petty professional jealousy."

"He probably would be—except for the most important thing of all—you're endowed, hopefully—" she allowed herself a tiny smile, "with normal sexual capabilities."

"Surely, Vic isn't handicapped in that respect."

Ilse toyed with her glass, reflective. "Adam, what I am about to say may seem disloyal to Vic or unethical or something, but I think it's necessary that I tell you in order to fully understand—"

The waitress was back with the drinks.

"Here you are, dollies," she said, setting the glasses down. "And when you're ready, you ought to try the prime ribs. They're terrif' tonight." She ambled away.

Adam lifted his drink. "You were saying—?"

"Vic's wife visited me some time ago—I never told Vic because he'd be furious, understandably. She wanted to meet the 'other woman', and was very frank about it. She bluntly asked if Vic was making it with me, and I'm not sure she believed me when I told her it was in no way that kind of relationship—nor did I want it to be. I admired Vic as a friend and enjoyed his company and conversation, and he seemed to need me only as someone to talk to, for the sense of warmth and understanding. Then she revealed that Vic hadn't slept with her for many years. Naturally, I began to wonder if Vic really lacked any physical interest in women— and if so, why did he at times seem to subtly encourage the rumors that I was his hot little bedmate."

"The poor bastard," Adam said softly.

"You think he's a hidden homo?"

"No. If he were a closet queen, he already has a wife for a cover-up. It's probably impotency—and he can't accept it."

"That could explain it."

"One thing puzzles me, and don't answer this if you don't want to—but if there was no sexual involve- ment—and you say you wanted none—why did you break up with him?"

Ilse twirled the stem of her glass abstractedly, frown- ing at the table. "I'm beginning to think it was subcon- ciously sexual after all. Vic's jealously possessive, and when he began noticing—or imagining—what he inter- preted as my attraction to you, he got very upset. Yes- terday when I quite innocently praised your surgical ability and asked why he didn't let you take over some of the major surgery cases, he was furious and said I must be blindly infatuated with you to suggest such an asinine thing. He ranted on like a jealous lover—really getting quite illogical for awhile—and as much as ordered me to stay away from you or our friendship was finished. I guess I should have been more sympathetic but I couldn't take being treated like chattel property, so I blew up too, and walked out."

"So it wasn't my charms, after all," he said ruefully.

"After last night," she said tartly, "I'm not so sure of my charms, either."

"Maybe we can console each other for our lacks."

"I'd rather console ourselves with what we don't lack. However, before I can expose my bruised ego to such a doubtful situation, I want to hear a complete and honest statement from you concerning that 'crime' you were contemplating earlier."

"To make it short, simple, and stupid—I'm thinking of disobeying direct orders and going ahead with Holly's operation on my own."

The sea-green eyes widened in disbelief. "You've got to be out of your mind! You'd never get away with it."

"After Vic leaves on his trip tomorrow, as his assistant I'll be nominally in charge of the surgical division. I could rush the operation through and not have to face the music until Vic gets back."

"He'd crucify you!"

"I know. That's why I called it a crime—against myself. Vic's already warned me that he's in a position to foul up my records and smear me with enough character damage so that no other hospital in the country would touch me. Even if I went into private practice, it'd be like starting all over again with two strikes against me. The black mark in my background would never wear off."

"Then how can you even consider anything that's bound to wreck your career?"

Adam shrugged and smiled at her. "There *is* a tiny ray of hope—if I succeeded in saving the kid, Vic's credibility would be knocked for a loop. He could no longer accuse me of being a second-rate surgeon, and I'd be in a stronger position to counter any character assassination he might attempt."

"Tiny ray of hope indeed! Virtually *nil*. Adam, you listen to me—" she leaned closer, eyes bright with intensity of feeling, "you've got a brilliant future ahead if you play it right. I know Vic—no matter how bad your hassle with him today, he'll get over it. He needs you badly, for one thing. If you do things *his* way, he'll even give you a pat on the head now and then."

"Sure—if I want to genuflect and kiss his ass every day."

"Just for another year, Adam—then you're free, with Vic's blessings. But if you cross him on something this important, he'll move mountains to crush you. You've got such a clear choice—"

"Yes, I have a clear choice—" Adam looked back at her with suddenly hot eyes, "but know what gets me? That kid—I keep seeing that cheerful, trusting little face—and she doesn't have one damn bit of choice."

Ilse drew away a bit, face expressionless, then looked down quickly and picked up her drink in a jerky, angry way.

"Now look—if that makes you sore—"

"I'm not sore—" she looked up again and he saw her eyes were wet and glistening, "it's only that I think I've fallen in love with a dumb, sweet big klutz without a future."

eleven

On the eve before his surgery, Atlee Northrup, Chairman of Amco Motors, lay unfed in bed and pleasantly drifting off in the haze of Nembutal fast darkening around him. A firm-jawed man of fifty-five with silver-streaked hair, Atlee was a picture of bronzed good health that looked out of place in a hospital. Although a bit overweight, he had the sturdy body of one who exercised every morning, golfed several afternoons a week, and aside from fairly heavy drinking and gourmet dining, always took good care of himself. The disorder that had laid him low was a large aneurysm in the thoracic portion of the aorta, to be surgically extirpated on the morrow and replaced with Dacron. Without such surgical intervention, his life expectancy would be two years at best—two years of dangling in a precarious state during which at any moment the lesion could rupture—bringing sudden, fatal, exsanguinating hemorrhage.

Atlee's impending date with the operating room was the cumulative result of five minutes of sensory joy experienced twenty-five years ago. A robust stud of thirty then and a rising star in the automotive industry who had already assured his future by marriage to the daughter of Amco's major stockholder, he was afflicted with a secret compulsion—to periodically wallow in sordid sexuality.

Doubtless contributing, albeit innocently, to Atlee's hidden carnality was his sweet and chaste wife, Christina, a delicate beauty who abhorred raw sex fully as much as Atlee loved it. She belonged to several esoteric, pseudo-religious groups that had helped her rationalize her defect of innate frigidity as a mystical superiority, one aspect of which was her belief that love could flower and the spirit soar only when freed of the body by steadfast denial of fleshly pleasures and prolonged periods of sexual abstinence. Thus she did little or nothing to alleviate Atlee's erotic tensions.

His favorite outlet, when the tensions became unbearable, was to hire three or four prostitutes (black girls were his preference) for an orgy involving all sorts of exotic positionings with each separately and intertangled with all of them together until driven almost out of his skull in a frenzy of sexuality lasting all night, or until whenever he was too satiated to continue.

Afterwards, feeling cleansed, he was able to go another two or three weeks as a hard-driving executive, model husband, pure-minded pillar of the church, and community leader. In civic affairs, one of his major contributions—perhaps as an expiatory sop to his secret guilts—was his forceful and successful opposition to the busing of black students into white schools in his own excluisve Bloomington Heights neighborhood.

Only once, to his knowledge, had he been burned— and that had been twenty-five years ago during the few minutes of sensory pleasure given to him by a sly-eyed young topless dancer (for fifty bucks) along with a dose of syph.

That had seemed no great problem. A very fine doctor, after confirming Atlee's fears of primary syphilis, gave him a single administration of 2,400,000 units of benzathine penicillin C (one-half injected in each buttock) which was considered adequate to knock out both primary and secondary syphilis. In a recheck a few months later, his STS—the serologic test for syphilis—was still seropositive but the doctor assured him this was normal with the majority of patients with early latent syphilis for more than a year after treatment and he could consider himself cured.

But he wasn't. A few of the tenacious microbes, perhaps of a resistant strain, remained latent but not dormant in his bloodstream, showing no discernible symptoms as they progressed into the "underground" phase—a phase that lab tests often fail to pick up. Proliferating as they went, the spirochetes continued their slow invasion. It was to take years, but sooner or later their ceaseless travels would surely bring them to one or more vulnerable points in the central nervous system, heart, arteries, brain, or other vital places where the degenerative reactions would begin.

In Atlee, the hidden foci began their erosions in the ascending portion of the aorta, eventually so weakening the walls of the thoracic part of the artery that it ballooned out to huge size under the driving pressure of blood directly from the heart. The aneurysm being painless, he might have died suddenly from its ultimate bursting without ever knowing of its existence had it not been for an associated encroachment upon the coronary orifices, which produced more tangible symptoms.

At first he blamed cigarettes for his growing cough and hoarseness—caused actually by paralysis of the recurrent laryngeal nerve, another effect of the syphilitic process. He also began experiencing a new difficulty in breathing and swallowing, and increasing back pain that came from erosion of the thoracic vertebrae. Deciding he needed a thorough check-up, he went to his good doctor friend, Victor Strang.

The diagnosis of a large thoracic aneurysm and coronary ostial stenosis shocked him. He would have been even more shocked had he known that the true medical designation—tactfully withheld from him— was syphilitic aortitis.

Ordered into a hospital bed at once, he was put on a course of 8,000,000 units of procaine penicillin G daily for a ten day period—sufficient to fully eradicate the syphilis and prevent further body damage—after which the operation could be performed.

Which was to be tomorrow forenoon . . .

And now, drifting off into the warm sybaritic haze of the barbiturate he had just taken, Atlee's subcurrent yearnings—freed of all conscious censorship—began forming into sinuous, enticing shapes . . . dark limbs, bosoms, undulating movements . . . The accumulating tensions of nearly two weeks of hospital rest with no sexual release added their own kind of chemical and psychic energy to the seductive visions growing in his head . . . the gleaming black nakedness . . . spread thighs . . . entangling limbs and rolling movement . . . his mouth roving, savoring the cosmetic-flavored faint saltiness of sweaty-slick hot flesh . . . trying to hold back but being sucked along faster and faster and deeper and deeper into those bottomless dark whirlpools of eternity.

He made a low moaning sound in his pre-sleep state and one hand, not consciously directed, slid down beneath the sheet to touch the growing hardness of his male organ.

"Are you feeling all right, Mr. Northrup?"

Through blurred vision he saw a face. Smiling . . . beautiful . . . Black . . .

"Come over here, honey," he said sleepily, reaching toward her with his arms, "and let's have a little fun."

Intern Donna Wheeler, who had just entered the room, looked at Nurse Nelda Frey in amused surprise.

"Does he mean you or me?"

Nelda, who was holding a tray, about to leave, glanced quickly at the prescribed white intern's jacket Donna was wearing with the little black badge pinned on the lapel for everyone to see: *Donna Wheeler, M.D., Intern Staff.*

"He's looking at you, Doctor," she said wryly. "I gave him a sedative awhile ago, and I thought he was asleep."

Atlee let out another sensual little groan. "Come on, girls . . . what're you waiting for?"

"What's he in for?" Donna said.

"Aneurysm."

"Oh wowie," Donna said softly. "We've got to get that blood pressure down. Can you get me some ice cubes? Fast."

"How many?"

"About a quart, in a towel."

Nelda hastened away and Donna approached the bed. His heavy-lidded eyes were fluttering now, not seeing her, and his words were unintelligible. He's in a dream state, she thought, and his head is full of it—the same kind of super-heated stuff that in virile young men often brings on a "wet dream" during the night— with all the metabolic increase and elevated blood pressure of regular sexual activity. What was the quickest drug for depressing him? She thought of calling a resident, but feared he would laugh at her. Besides, this was the last of the twenty-eight patients she'd been assigned to for today, and she wanted to make a good record. The heavy body writhed slowly, suggestively.

"You just wait a bit," she crooned, stroking the patient's head, "and we'll take care of you."

Nelda appeared with the ice cubes.

"Thanks," said Donna, and first drawing the bedsheet down below the patient's knees, took the towel full of ice cubes and gently but firmly pressed it against the male organ that was heroically jutting up like a tentpole beneath the hospital nightgown. Northrup let out an aggrieved moan and tried to roll away, but Donna held the ice pack firmly in place.

Nelda started giggling.

"That ought to cool him," said Donna. "We can't risk his blood pressure blowing the aneurysm, can we?"

twelve

Natalie had finished the last letter and placed it on the bedside stand when the nurse came in.

"It's time for your sleeping pill, Mrs. Tyler," said the nurse, holding out a single tablet on a tray.

"Just put it on the stand, Miss Burns. I'll take it in a few moments."

"Would you care for another Demerol first? Your limit's been lifted, you know, so . . ."

"Thanks, but I won't need it. I'm really feeling much better." There was no need to tell Miss Burns that Demerol no longer helped.

"I'm so glad. You *do* look . . . more at peace. Will you be wanting anything else before you go to sleep?"

"Not a thing. I'm just looking forward to a nice long rest."

"Good night, Mrs. Tyler."

"Good night, Miss Burns."

Alone, she left the sleeping pill untouched and concentrated once again on the problem. She knew she had reached the fringes of that no-man's-land between life and death and the only question now was how long would it take to cross over. Days? weeks? Months?

It was no longer the thought of dying that she found hard to take. Not even the pain (which was far worse.). The most dreaded thought of all was that of the evil finally becoming seeded in her brain to begin eating away at the only thing she still had left. She remembered an uncle who had died of lung cancer, but not until after it had reached the brain and turned him childish, babbling out silly words, reduced him almost to the primal vegetable state before the final reprieve of death.

That was the most unbearable thought of all—the lost control over one's thinking, of awareness of what was happening, being completely at the mercy of the greedy virus within and the well-meaning but all too often unthinking sympathy of those around her. What a travesty of human love to keep the miserable remnants of one's body alive beyond that point—the brain wrecked and gone, the body useless. What a nightmarish affront to human dignity!

And more than that—the wrenching, agonized pain of those who loved you—Dave who sat there waiting, waiting, emotionally handcuffed. In every way handcuffed, unable to do a thing.

They shoot horses, but not people.

And along with that, the endless drain of money. Dave would be struggling to get out from under their burden of debts for many years to come. Debts that were still snowballing.

All for what? Only to hold off for a little longer that crossover to the other dark shore. To prolong her agony. Dave's agony.

She had often wondered when one reaches the point when the death ahead is preferable to the life of the moment—and had known she'd reached that point yesterday when they wheeled her back into the hospital. The doctors knew, too, but wouldn't tell her anything. They were so kind—professionally kind—and so were the nurses. But still they wouldn't tell her blunt facts. Like how much time she had left. The answers were always vague and cheery with false hopes.

All she had left was her still-intact brain. The capacity to think, evaluate.

And make decisions.

Another wave of pain began grinding through her and she gritted her teeth against it, determined never to scream again.

It lasted for several minutes this time. She turned half on her side, hands clenched, fingernails cutting into her palms, her face clenched up tightly as her little fists. Slowly it subsided.

Forcing herself to sit up, she reached for the water decanter and poured a glass beside it full. It was time to sleep.

"I love you, Dave," she whispered, raising the glass and thinking, my God, woman, you don't have to cry about it! Her other hand had already extracted from beneath the pillow case the little plastic bottle of barbiturate tablets she'd stolen from Dave's jacket pocket during their goodbye kiss.

Emptying all the pills into one palm, she dutifully swallowed each of them with a chaser of water, one by one.

Adam lay on his side, one naked limb still entangled with the other naked limbs, an arm around the satiny torso, a hand caressing the warm dampness of her back. He was still hot and sweaty, but wondrously relaxed, blissfully happy. It had been indescribably good.

Her lips, close to his, murmured, "Do you feel like I do, darling? What are your thoughts?"

"That life is pretty damned wonderful, and—" something suddenly connected in his brain and he drew back slightly.

"Is anything wrong?"

"I've just decided to operate on the kid."

She laughed softly. "But darling, you made that decision hours ago."

"Not really. I wasn't sure I had the guts to go through with it until now. And Christ, there are still a million preparations to squeeze in somehow."

"But not in the middle of the night, darling. Both of us are going to have a long, hard day tomorrow, so now I think we should just relax."

"You're absolutely right," he said, and turned toward her again, his lips eagerly seeking hers.

At about 2:30 A.M., the floor nurse peeked through the door at Natalie Tyler, and relieved to see that she was sleeping peacefully, continued on her rounds.

At 4:23 A.M., the ICU nurse, on instructions from the intern on duty, began methodically disconnecting all the various leads and appurtenances attached to the body of Speed Wilson, after which she drew the sheet over his head and went to the nearest phone to call in her death report to the supervising night nurse.

thirteen

Shortly after 8:00 a.m., just beginning her rounds, Kerri Kozak arrived at Private Room 403 and was shocked to discover a new tenant—a querulous old woman, obviously rich because a glittering big diamond ring on one skinny finger had not yet been removed—was being installed.

Responding to her questioning expression, one of the two nurses who had just finished moving the woman from a wheel chair into the bed, beckoned to Kerri to come outside with her.

"Where's Mrs. Tyler?" Kerri said.

"She passed away during the night," the nurse said crisply, and handed Kerri a sealed envelope. "She left this for you."

Wet-eyed, Kerri opened the envelope and began reading:

"My dear friend, Kerri,

"What I am about to ask may seem outrageous,

*but you will not dare refuse, because (ha, ha) you
know that death wishes must be respected.*

*"My biggest worry, as you know, is my sweet
Dave. I fear terribly for him that first day after
I'm gone, so-ooo—as the very last favor I shall
ever ask of you—no, not just asking, I'm BEG-
GING—you simply MUST not let Dave be alone
tonight! Both of our families live on opposite sides
of the country and won't be able to get here for
another day. Dave will want to be alone, but I've
ORDERED him to call you for a date—and if he
forgets, call HIM. Forget all the conventional garbage about how people are supposed to show
grief—I'm the guy dead, aren't I? Have dinner
and a few drinks with him. Make him smile, make
him laugh. Even flirt with him—and I hope he
flirts back (the rat!)—anything to keep his
thoughts away from dismal me.*

*"Now remember I am depending on you, dear
friend, and knowing that you will help him
through the first horrible day makes it possible for
me to die a little bit happier.*

"Goodbye sweet Kerri, and God bless you,

Natalie"

Folding the letter back into its envelope, Kerri went
off to the nurse's rest room, where she could stop her
tears and repair her make-up.

At 11:46 A.M., Adam stripped off his surgical gloves
and tossed them in the waste "kick bucket" on its
wheeled stand and watched Atlee Northrup being
rolled out of the operating room. The operation had run
nearly a half hour longer than it should have, but otherwise seemed to have gone well. Victor Strang, although
working with undue slowness, had shown his old meticulous skill in not only performing the difficult feat of ex-

cising the large thoracic aneurysm and replacing the diseased section of aorta with Dacron, but had also accom-
plished the extremely ticklish procedure of repairing the
disease-narrowed coronary orifice at the heart itself.
This would dramatically relieve blood pressure and
improve circulation.

That is, if the surgery held up long enough for the
natural healing process to take over with its additional
strengthening.

Strang himself had shown not the slightest doubts.
Before leaving about fifteen minutes ago—immediately
after ordering the patient off the pump and his chest
closed—he had glanced at Adam with a mocking little
smile, as if to say, *"Fault this one if you can."*

Ilse Jensen came up beside Adam as he was walking
out. "How do you think it went this time?"

"I'm keeping my fingers crossed."

She was silent until they were walking in the corridor. Then, "I'm full of a lot of silly, unprofessional
little urges today. For example, like wishing I could
reach out and hold your hand—which of course would
start a whole new rash of rumors."

"I'm full of a lot more unprofessional urges than just
holding hands—but I agree this is no time and place
for that kind of nonsense."

"Adam . . ." She was hesitant, reflective. "I don't
want you to think I might be trying to, you know—
snare you into any emotional entanglement such as
marriage or any other kind of commitment. I value my
freedom and respect yours. Last night was marvelous,
and I hope there will be others—but I have no demands or expectations."

"You're saying the right words," Adam said, grinning at her, "but I don't fully believe you. However, as
a basis for our future relationship, how could any male
chauvinist pig object?"

"Don't tempt me to start eating my own words, Doctor," she said tartly.

"How about eating lunch with me instead? Dutch, of course, or we can flip coins. Then we can discuss the Big Caper."

"Adam—I'm scared of what's going to happen to you when Vic finds out."

"I won't have to worry about that before tomorrow. Vic's personal car and driver were waiting for him outside. By now he's on the way to the airport, and will soon be soaring on his way to all the glories awaiting him at the Association meeting in Chicago."

"How soon do you think we can get the operation started?"

Adam frowned. "There won't be an operating room available before six. Add another couple hours to get things set up and it'll be eight, at least, before we can get going. But there's still the unsolved matter of the blood. We'll need about fifteen 500 cc bottles—half fresh, half stored. You know how expensive that is. I had another talk with Holly's parents and found out they don't have any medical coverage—the guy runs a failing garage business, due to a big chain gas station that moved in across the street, and couldn't keep up the payments. They had no idea that with all the hospital expenses added in, an operation like this runs from $4,000 to $5,000. I'm waiving the surgical fee, and I think I can cover for most of the other expenses, but the blood is a big item, cash on the line."

"Apparently you never realized how versatile I am, Doctor," Ilse said, smiling. "Vic has always depended on me to doublecheck the blood situation, so I already knew the problem—and have taken steps to solve it."

"Like what?"

"Mrs. Robbins happens to be a devout churchgoer, so with a little blarney, I induced the officer in charge of our own blood bank to contact the minister of her church, who has promised to line up fifteen donors who'll contribute a pint of blood each to the regional Red Cross center near her hometown. The credits will be transferred here for whatever type blood Holly needs. If they have trouble getting all they need, I think I can scare up a few more donors right here in the hospital, myself included."

"My God—for that, I'll buy your lunch, and dinner too!"

"No. We'll flip coins. I seem to be getting hooked on gambling."

fourteen

The naked black body couldn't have cared less that the white, porcelain-topped table on which it lay was ice cold and surrounded by a small circle of observers. William "Speed" Wilson had departed from this world nearly twelve hours ago, and the dead protoplasm composing the fleshly temple wherein had once dwelt his soul—or at least his physiological and psychological functioning centers—was already far advanced in the muscle-stiffening process of rigor mortis.

Sergeant Borman, who had just come into the chill, macabre atmosphere of the morgue dissection room, glanced at the corpse and then at Loren Cass, a first year resident who was making notes on the autopsy forms attached to a clipboard.

"You the doc who's doing the autopsy?" said Borman.

"Nope. I'm just an unhappy future gynecologist temporarily assigned to the morgue to expand my awareness of the futility of delivering so many cute little babies into the world."

Borman looked at the others—a reporter he knew from a Detroit paper and several interns and nurses who, as part of their education, were periodically required to watch a post-mortem. Who's in charge here?"

"Dr. Furtig," said Cass.

"When's he due?"

"He might come toddling in just before dinnertime to work up his evening appetite. On the other hand, he could come running, like a half hour ago, if he finds out he's got a couple of gorgeous chicks in the audience." The nurses giggled.

Encouraged, Cass leaned toward the corpse. "Now let's take a look at the molars." Making a great show of it, he pried open the stiff jaw. "Wowie—did you ever see a prettier set? Fine calcification, no periodontal problems except for one bicuspid knocked out, and—oh my, one solid gold filling—no doubt from too many tootsie rolls as a kid."

Unamused, Borman frowned at Jack Barnes, the reporter. "What the hell you here for?"

"Same reason you are, Sergeant. You picked up two guys carrying handguns. Right? But you can't prove they're the same guys and the same guns that killed Wilson until you get the calibre of the slugs and see if they match the guns. Right?"

"Where do you pick up all that crap?"

"I don't want to get arrested for refusing to divulge the source of my crap, so let's just say I keep my ears to the ground."

Disgusted, Borman shifted his attention to a wheeled cart that had suddenly appeared, pushed by the morgue *diener,* Clem Jackson. Stuffing the remnants of a late sugared doughnut into his mouth, Jackson hurriedly began taking instruments from the cart and laying them out on a stainless steel stand beside the dissecting table.

The reason for his haste was Dr. Otto Furtig, who had arrived a few moments before and was standing just inside the door staring in mild surprise at the assemblage.

"Well, well," he said grumpily, "I wasn't advised that this was to be a tv spectacular," and then noting the two nurses, his manner transformed into joviality as he strode briskly toward the autopsy table. Constructed like a small ox—wide-shouldered, heavy-muscled, and no more than five feet five inches high—the pathology chief exuded virility, even though the fringe of hair showing beneath his cap was almost white. He directed the stabbing blackness of his eyes at Cass. "How's our patient coming along?"

"No complaints from him yet," said Cass dutifully.

"Give him a chance," said Furtig, reaching for the clipboard. "We haven't started on him yet."

While he studied the details of the case on the clipboard, the *diener* finished laying out the knives, rib cutters, forceps, and power saw for the skull—all of them clean but not autoclaved as they would have to be for use in the operating rooms above. Sterility was not necessary for the dead.

"This is a medical examiner's case," said Furtig, handing back the clipboard, "so he gets the whole works." Thrusting out a powerful arm, he slid into the long plastic-coated apron that Jackson was holding ready for him, then powdered his hands and slipped on rubber gloves.

"Now some of you may find this abhorrent and revolting to watch," he said with a sly grin at the nurses as he picked up a knife, "but I want to assure you it's beautiful—beautiful because it's truth—the ultimate truth. Whenever any of the eighty-seven brilliant doctors in this mighty hospital get stumped—which is frequent—they come running down to Pathology to find out what's wrong. The Pathologist alone sees all, knows all, and his diagnosis never errs."

"Any customer not fully satisfied," added Cass, "can apply at the admissions office and get his money back."

"The primary concern of Pathology, of course," Furtig went on, slightly irked, "is not to function as a check-out point for our flood of satisfied customers— but to keep them out of here for as long as possible. To that end, Pathology tests a patient's blood, checks his excrement, identifies infections, decides whether a tumor is benign or malignant, and advises the patient's physician about the disease. There are always a few doctors, unfortunately, who don't come to us until it's too late, if at all. There are others who are very careless in their note-taking. For example . . ."

Reaching out, he grasped the stiffened left arm of the corpse and with a powerful, twisting motion bent it back.

"Do you see that?" with the tip of the knife held in his other hand, he traced a series of raised markings on the inner section of arm." Junkie tracks. The basilic and cephalic veins have been popped so many times they're collapsing, drying up. Yet none of our doctors in EW, ICU or down here seems to have made any note of it in the case history or autopsy forms."

"Uh, I hadn't finished my notes, Dr. Furtig," said Cass.

"Maybe because you were too busy hamming it up for the ladies?"

"Yes sir," Cass said humbly, "but in the future I'll strive to emulate your example."

"Try emulating this sometime." Furtig bent over the body and again a powerful arm snaked out, the knife flashing. With two strong strokes he incised from each shoulder to a point at the bottom of the chest, and then with a third stroke—making a soft, tearing sound, a slight hissing—sliced the belly open from the chest to the genitals. One of the nurses gagged into her hands and scampered from the room.

Furtig continued, working swiftly, first peeling back the chest flap and cutting the flesh loose from the ribs with a heavier knife, then with the big, sharp rib-cutters, cutting through the rib cage to the pericardium and lungs. Blood stained the instruments and gloved hands of the path chief, and a sweetish stench was beginning to be noticeable. Continuing downward, he cut back the lower flaps of belly until the abdomen was open. Cass, meanwhile had turned on the suction hose and was syphoning blood from the abdomen and chest.

"Hah—!" said Furtig. "Look at that liver—see how it's swollen and spotty from hemorrhage? That's hepatitis—from dirty needles. I'll bet a nickel we find damage started on the heart, too." Skillfully, he excised the enlarged liver and dumped it into a pail beside the corpse.

"Excuse me, Doc'," said the sergeant. "How long do you think it'll take to dig those slugs out for me?"

The path chief stared at Borman as if seeing him for the first time. "What's the rush? Since this case comes under the jurisdiction of the law, making a complete autopsy mandatory, it may take a long time—depending on where the bullets are located."

"No offense, Doc'. I can wait."

The gloved hands went back to exploring, the scalpel moving with skillful, deft strokes. Intestines, stomach, kidneys, bits of sample tissues sliced from here and there, joined the accumulating organs in the bucket.

"Now here's something to behold—the soul itself." Furtig had excised the heart and held up the glistening, purplish-red object for all to see. "Note the swelling of infection around the valve—rotten at the core, you might say. Even without the bullets and dirty needles, this guy would have been joining his ancestors very prematurely. The heroin was killing him fast. I'll be interested in seeing what it's done to his brain."

Tossing the heart into the pail with a dull, plopping

sound, he vigorously continued plundering the body, and moments later removed a large, spongy mass of lung, which he dumped splatteringly on the drainage table. Using a thin, sharp knife, he began slicing through it methodically, as one would slice bologna. The knife stopped suddenly against hardness.

"Exhibit number one." With forceps, he extracted a small object. "From the lower lobe of the right lung."

"That one of the slugs?" said the sergeant.

Furtig handed the bullet to Cass. "Wash it off and give it to the officer to identify for himself. I wouldn't presume to infringe on another man's profession."

The resident rinsed and wiped the bullet and tossed it to the sergeant, who examined it with satisfaction. "Caliber .38," he said. "German made."

"Sergeant, that's fantastic," the reporter said admiringly. "How can you tell so much about the bullet right off the bat?"

"Expertise—" Borman's tone was self-deprecating—"just plain professional expertise. Guy who's had all the gun exposure I get, learns a few things. Overseas in the MPs during World War II, we used to confiscate just about every type of gun and ammunition there is—German, French, Italian, Spanish, Russian—you name it. Fool around with enough of them, like I did, you get to notice all the little ways they're different. Some are works of art, some just plain crap. Take this for example—" he juggled the slug in his palm—"this was shot from an old P-38—that was the German Saturday night special back then. Funny how the krauts could make pretty guns like Lugers and Walthers and then stoop to turning out production like crap like the P-38. Shoot 'em a few hundred times, they'll blow up in your face. The G.I.s brought 'em back by the thousands and most of them are still floating around the country, unregistered."

"Maybe the krauts planned it that way," suggested

Cass, "as a long-range way of blowing off a lot of American heads after the war ended."

"Wouldn't put it past them," said Borman, who himself was of German ancestry. "They got smarts, them krauts."

The pathologist made a grunting sound. "Here's another one—just a little one imbedded in the scapula. I'll bet it nicked a vein on the way through. There was a lot of bleeding in the chest." Getting the little slug dug out, he passed it to Cass, who in turn cleansed it and tossed it to the sergeant.

"Walther .25 caliber," Borman said authoritatively, obviously pleased. He didn't bother to explain that his expertise was immeasurably aided by the fact that the two handguns taken from the suspected killers had been a Walther and a P-38.

Furtig beckoned to his resident assistant. "Examine the chest cavity and tell me what it looks like to you."

Cass craned his neck and peered in. "Do I have to use explicit language in front of the ladies?"

"All that blood had to come from somewhere. Can you find the leak?"

Clued, Cass looked more carefully. "Looks like something tore through one side of the subclavian vein."

"Right. That's why our patient never got out of shock. He died of hemorrhage. If they'd really been on the ball upstairs, they might have saved him. As it was, all that blood and plasma they poured into him was just wasted."

"So what's another couple hundred dollars down the drain?" Cass said lightly. "One thing the medical profession never has to worry about is money."

Quietly, Mike Tunstra eased the dissection room door open and peered in. The reason for the orderly's

stealth was that he was a good half hour late and hoped
to slip in without being noticed by the path chief, who
had ordered him to be on hand to help during the autopsy. It wasn't normally part of Mike's job but they
were shorthanded because last night the path technician
had been fired, and orderlies were expected to fill in
wherever they were needed.

For the crud work, that is. Mike detested the sight
and smell of gooey, gloppy, bloody guts and organs
hauled out of dead bodies and had deliberately goofed
off in the coffee shop as long as he dared, hoping that
in the meantime the *diener* would get stuck with most
of the gory clean-up chores. Old Furtig might get sore,
but the worst he could do to him was chew his ass off.

Mike grinned, remembering the reaming the path
technician had got the other night. They'd found out
he'd been lifting morphine from hospital supplies—
thinking he was clever by hiding it in a little plastic tube
shaped like a cigar and shoved up his rectum—the
same trick used by a lot of prisoners for hiding their
bread—except in this case, one of the police dogs had
really chewed his ass half off trying to get at the morphine, so now the jerk was in jail wearing it in a sling.

He was still in the doorway, peering past old Furtig's
back, when the brainstorm hit him. It came like a little
Fourth-of-July sparkler suddenly bursting into joyful
incandescence in his brain—touched off by a gruesome
glimpse of the bloodied belly and chest of the corpse
gaping wide open.

In that instant, the problem that had been bugging
the hell out of Mike for the past twenty-four hours—
how to smuggle the packages of heroin out of the hospital—was solved. A solution both simple and perfect.

Then, in the next moment, spotting the obnoxious
face of Sergeant Borman, Mike quickly backed out of
the doorway and eased the door shut again. He sure as
hell didn't want to invite any further attention from

that uniformed pig, who despite not having the brains of an ape, had the instincts of a bloodhound and was already too suspicious. He could always fake a gut-ache for not showing up at the autopsy, and there wasn't a doctor in the hospital, except maybe old Barr, who could tell he was faking it. He might even get prescribed a slug of hospital booze.

Hurrying toward the locker area, where he intended to keep a low profile until after the sergeant was gone, he felt far more elated than booze could ever make him—more like the high after blowing a good stick of grass. By playing it cool, by not falling for that horseshit about a hospital shakedown—he would soon be loaded, but *loaded*.

Man, it was beautiful! Ready-made for him. Part of his job was to help at the loading ramp where the meat was heisted into the morticians' hearses. The schedules giving names of the deceased, the time of pick-up, and the mortuary that would be picking them up, were tacked up on a bulletin board beside the door. The undertakers, always so anxious to get their meat, were never late. In Speed's case, however, no relatives or friends had shown up to claim the body, so a police meat wagon was scheduled to come around in the morning to haul Speed off to a pauper's grave in an unpainted wooden box for which the county would be billed about fifty bucks. What a gasser! Mike began giggling, a bit hysterically, from the sheer beautiful zaniness of it.

For inside that cruddy wooden box would be a millionaire—Speed with his chest and belly packed with nearly three million bucks worth of H. Who ever said you couldn't take it with you?

His giggling stopped abruptly. That, of course, was the catch, the bigger of the two big problems not yet solved. The lesser problem—getting the plastic bags into the hollow spaces of chest and belly, and the corpse sewed up again—he was sure he could manage that somehow.

But after that—after the body was safely past the police blockade and headed for the graveyard—how was he going to get the H back again?

The floor supervising nurse stuck her head into the nurses' lounge. "Miss Kozak," she called, "telephone for you—the one on my desk."

Kerri, about to go off duty, felt a nervous sensation clutch at her throat. She was positive it would be Dave Tyler. All afternoon she had tried to summon enough courage to call him, as Natalie had requested in her note, but kept putting it off in the hope that he would call her first.

"Thank you, Miss Palmer," she said, and hastened away.

All day, Kerri had been haunted by the tragedy of Natalie, which she was sure had been ended by suicide, although there had been no official mention of it, and probably wouldn't be.

Under the same circumstances, she wondered, would she have the courage to take her own life?

The more she thought about it, the clearer it seemed that there was a lot more involved than just courage—or perhaps courage was just another name for the same thing—that thing being love.

What a wonderful thing—to love! Even when dying, in deepest pain, Natalie's thoughts had been more for Dave than for herself. It added a nobility, a true grace, to the terribleness of her death.

For Kerri, that was the impossible dream—to love a man totally. She yearned for male love, and *wanted* to love back. She enjoyed male company and often was strongly attracted, but the moment the scene grew too warm—the touch of his hand in a certain way, the sensed expectancy of kisses, and more—when the vibrations from the guy only too clearly conveyed his *wanting something from her,* she was turned off. From deep within her, always, flooded up that formless animal fear and she just couldn't, *couldn't* let herself go.

She knew, but didn't understand why, that it was all linked in some way to that dark, nightmarish episode back in high school—now so tightly curtained off in her memory that she no longer could remember exactly what had happened and was stubbornly determined never to try to remember.

Picking up the phone on Miss Palmer's desk, she was surprised to find the caller was Detective Jerry London.

"My deductive efforts," he told her, "have uncovered the facts that your work day is about over and that you're not wearing a wedding ring. Projecting from that solid basis into wild but delightful theory, I am wondering if you would care to join me for dinner tonight?"

This time she felt a definite thrill race up her spine. She wanted to say 'yes', if only to escape the obligation Natalie had thrust upon her, but she just couldn't.

"I'd really love to go, but I—I already have a commitment for this evening," she said.

"Clue me," he said. "Are your evening commitments running quite heavy, or should I try again?"

"Oh, by all means—" she was afraid she was sounding too eager, "I have a lot of free evenings."

"How about tomorrow, then?"

"I'd love to."

The time and place were set, and she hung up feeling quite gay—until remembering the depressive duty she still faced for tonight.

Getting out the slip of paper on which she had jotted Dave's address and telephone number, she nervously began dialing.

fifteen

Dr. Hugo Barr was on the telephone when Glenna Woods rushed into his office.

"Oh Dr. Barr—Dr. Barr—!"

The medical director frowned and raised a hand to silence her. It was after 7:00 P.M., and normally his secretary, who had left at five, would have protected him from such an unseemly interruption. Cupping the phone with one hand, he said snappishly, "Miss Woods, whatever it is will have to wait. I'm in the middle of a phone consultation."

Flushing a bit, Glenna waited with folded arms while Barr spoke again into the phone: "As I was saying, Dr. Hatfield, the other day you sent over to our clinic a young lady, a Mrs. Claiborne, for tuberculosis treatment..."

"Excuse me, Dr. Barr," Hatfield said a bit impatiently, "but I wonder if we can't postpone this discussion until tomorrow. I was just about to leave for a dinner engagement, and I'm already late." Dr. Scott Hat-

field was a fashionable private physician, very successful and secure.

"I understand your haste, Dr. Hatfield. You operate
a financially successful enterprise. You carry a case
load of nearly two hundred patients a week and put in
ten-hour days—excluding evenings, weekends, and all
day on Wednesdays when you're out playing golf, at
which times you are completely unavailable. Your hard
work nets you $70,000 or more per annum. In defer-
ence to your heavy workload, I'll try to be brief, but I
cannot delay this matter."

"At your service, Doctor," Hatfield said politely. He
was well aware—and like all private physicians resented
the fact—that the hospital clinic with its far superior diagnostic and treatment facilities on which the physicans
depended—did not have to accept every patient sent
there.

"The patient you have sent us is being studied for
bowel and kidney disorders as well as the tuberculosis.
On checking the files, I find that we received only the
chest X-rays. We want to see all your X-rays and test
findings."

"What do you want all that stuff for? I'm handling the
bowel and kidney disorders. You're only taking care of
the tuberculosis."

One of Barr's basic tenets was that illness could be
treated only in terms of the totality of a person. To
treat one specific area of a patient without taking the
entire person into account, he preached to his interns,
"can be as wasteful as repairing the heating system of a
house that has no door."

"Very well, Dr. Hatfield. We'll accept the patient on
those terms. We'll return her in the morning so you can
just send us back the lungs and keep the rest of the
body."

"All right, Dr. Barr—I'll send over the rest of the
data as soon as my office opens tomorrow."

Hanging up, the medical director looked grumpily at Glenna. "Miss Woods, in view of our Emergency Ward and all our excellent doctors available for life and death matters, what in the world can be so important as to impel you to call on a tired and cranky old doctor who at this moment couldn't be entrusted to apply a bandaid?"

"There's something going on that I think you ought to know about, Doctor. OR-4 is getting set up for an operation that wasn't scheduled or approved by Dr. Strang, and since Dr. Strang is away on a trip, I felt I should report it directly to you."

"Why me? Isn't Dr. Cane second in command over the surgical division?"

"Well, yes—but I happened to overhear Dr. Strang and Dr. Cane discussing the case. Dr. Strang very, *very* strongly and specifically ordered Dr. Cane not to go ahead with that operation, and that's why I think you ought to stop it right away!"

Barr looked long and steadily at the flushed, overly-tense woman, then smiled. "My dear young lady," he said gently, "I will suggest two courses of action. First, in the event of any future eavesdropping, keep it strictly to yourself. Two, go home and relax and try to seek a little insight into your own motivations."

sixteen

At 8:02 p.m., Holly Robbins, whimpering softly, was rolled on a wheeled stretcher from the induction room into Operating Room 4, where she would remain for the next two to three hours, and more likely than not—according to the heavy odds against her—die there. But this she did not know. Like most children, her fears were not of that mystical, storybook thing called Death, but solely a reaction to all the mysterious needles and knives that her lively imagination—despite reassuring briefings from doctors and nurses—had depicted as waiting to descend on her tender young body.

As the stretcher rolled silently over the floor, which was of a special electric-conducting composition to prevent any slight spark of static electricity that could touch off an explosion of the highly inflammable anesthesia gases, Holly's eyes roved over the strange, windowless walls of grayish-green ceramic tiles. Although slightly sedated with Nembutal and Demerol, she was still wide awake and curious. To shorten the period of anesthesia, since her operation was to be a long one, she would not be put to sleep until almost the last moment. Suddenly she noticed the large plastic dome in the ceiling.

"What's that window in the ceiling for?" she said suspiciously.

"That's the observation dome. There's a little room up there so medical students and visiting doctors can watch."

"Watch *me?*" Holly was horrified. "Won't I be naked?"

"Only a small section of your torso. Your head and all the rest of you from the tummy down will be completely covered."

Now aware of the half dozen other people in the room—all of them garbed in scrub greens, heads capped and faces masked so that little more than their eyes could be seen—Holly said, "What are all these people doing here?"

"Well, the two on your left are the doctor and the technician who run the heart-lung machine, and way behind you is the assistant anesthesiologist who's responsible for the anesthesia machine and the EEG recorder, and over there are the first and second instrument nurses and the circulating nurse. Some of them have already been here for a couple hours getting things ready. The rest will be along soon. All told, there'll be twelve on the operating team."

"Twelve people just for my operation?"

"That's right."

"Wowie!"

The stretcher had reached the operating table. "Now hold on to your sheet," said the nurse, "and see if you can help the orderly and me hoist you over to the table."

"Okay." Some of the safety-in-numbers psychology

was calming Holly, and besides, she was getting drowsy.

On the operating table, she looked up to see a large pair of horn-rimmed spectacles peering down at her.

"Hello, Holly," said a gruff, kindly voice. "I'm Dr. Langsteen." The masked man bent and blotted her perspiring face. "Before we put you to sleep, there are still a few things we have to do."

"Will they hurt?"

"Not a bit. All we want is to put this cuff on an arm so we can get readings of your blood pressure, and this plate we'll strap on a leg—" he showed her a silver electrode with a lead to the cautery machine, "and then we'll put a little tube into one of your ankle veins to keep you supplied with blood and medications. It's so painless, you won't even know we're doing it."

He signaled Jim Bolan, one of the interns, who using a brush and germicidal soap, thoroughly scrubbed Holly's left ankle. Langsteen then swabbed the same spot with an orange antiseptic, and with a syringe handed to him by a waiting nurse, injected the area with Novocain.

Holly tried to watch what was going on, but Langsteen had skillfully bunched sterile towels up around her leg to block her view, and the nurse had moved around with a restraining hand to keep her from sitting up.

"Miss Vladek," said Langsteen as he began the cutdown into the large saphenous vein, "why don't you explain to Holly how the heart-lung machine over there will do all the work for her heart and lungs while we're repairing her heart. I'll bet she'd like to know all about it so she can tell her friends later."

"Sure. See that tall glass column, Holly?" Falling for the bait, Holly twisted her head around to look. "That's the container for your blood after it's pumped out of your veins. Then oxygen gets bubbled into it, just like your lungs would do it, and after that the bubbles have to be taken out again by the debubbler—that's the slanting tube on top. After that it gets pumped through a water bath to keep it exactly the right temperature and then back into your arteries. It's really quite simple."

Meanwhile, Langsteen had opened a vein and was pushing a thin, flexible catheter up through the vein into the abdomen—a procedure that Holly could not feel in the slightest—where it would remain throughout the operation for drawing blood samples and introducing drugs into the bloodstream.

He was about finished when Dr. Joe Oberholtzer lumbered in.

"Well, well," he boomed, "so this is the star of the show. I must say we've got a real beauty this time."

Although heavy-lidded and drowsy, Holly blushed. "Who're you?"

"I'm the anesthetist. Some people who like bigger words call me the anesthesiologist. Either way won't offend me. I'm the guy who's going to put you to sleep."

"I'm already hardly able to stay awake."

"Good. We'll help it along, but first—" he held up a black oxygen mask, "I'm going to give you a little pure oxygen—the same stuff they give athletes to make them win at the Olympics. I'll put this over your face and I want you to just breathe normally."

As Holly began breathing through the mask, he gave her an injection of thiopentone, a barbiturate that put her to sleep almost immediately. From then on, for the next two or three hours, Holly's life would depend on the skill and care with which he performed his job, for in modern surgery the anesthetist had become, in effect, the caretaker as well as the physiological bookkeeper of the sleeping body. Using as few drugs as possible, he protects the patient from surgical trauma and damage. He is also responsible for checking blood pressure, venous pressure, control of respiration, acid level, pulse rate, urine output, and cerebral reflexes. Without a highly trained anesthesiologist, major heart surgery would not be possible.

After a few moments, Oberholtzer gave an injection of Scoline, a relaxant which would paralyze the muscles—including Holly's ability to breathe. Satisfied that she now had enough extra oxygen in her system to sustain her for at least a minute without breathing, he took off the mask and quickly slipped an endotracheal tube through her mouth and down her throat almost to the carina, or point where the windpipe separates for the two lungs. The other end of the tube was hooked to a black bag which the assistant anesthetist began squeezing, like a bellows, at a rate of about forty times a minute, thus manually doing the work of Holly's lungs and pumping into them a mixture of oxygen, nitrous oxide, and halothane—a combination that would keep her asleep and shielded from pain.

All this took about one minute. The paralyzing effects of the Scoline would last another two minutes— enough time for Oberholtzer to insert a slender nasalgastric tube into Holly's left nostril and thread it down into her stomach. This would serve as an air vent to prevent overinflation and draw off accumulated secretions that might be burped up or inhaled into the lungs.

"The Scoline should be wearing off by now, Herb," said Oberholtzer. "Put her on the Bird and help me finish up before Adam comes charging in."

The resident anesthetist stopped the hand pumping and hooked the tube to the automatic Bird respirator.

While Herb inserted a pair of needles into the skin of Holly's scalp to pick up her brain waves as a check on the anesthesia and the efficiency of the heart-lung machine, Oberholtzer inserted a needle with a tube attached into each forearm, providing intravenous entry into the body for plasmalyte, a balanced salt solution to keep the veins open. Next a thin catheter was inserted up the urethra into the bladder and the other end of it joined by rubber tube to a bottle on the floor, allowing a constant check on the urine flow—an important parameter of blood perfusion throughout the body. An electric thermometer was placed in the rectum to give continuous readings of rectal temperature, and another one was inserted through the mouth down into the esophagus near the heart to give approximate readings of internal temperatures needed by the heart-lung technician as a guide during the cooling and re-warming of the patient's blood.

During all this, the nurses were deftly active, laying out instruments, preparing the drugs that would be needed, taping electric leads to the floor. One had begun scrubbing Holly from neck to tummy with warm water and germicidal soap. Another ran a bandage around Holly's waist and secured both arms and knees to the table with straps to prevent her from slipping off.

At 8:56 p.m., Adam walked in with Don Wolff, who would be first assisting with the surgery. Wolff glancing at the operating room clock, raised his eyebrows.

"My God, Adam," he said, "look how these beavers are racing around. They're four minutes ahead of schedule."

"Then I guess we'd better get started."

Two of the nurses—one of them Ilse Jensen—helped the surgeons into their gowns and gloves, and they walked over to the table. Under the glare of operating lights, the nude body was a garish, glistening orange from the antiseptic that had been painted on it from neck to thighs, then covered with Steridrape, a sterile, transparent adhesive plastic covering. A resident had begun the final step of draping Holly's body with green toweling, leaving only the chest and upper stomach exposed for surgery.

Adam glanced around. The entire team was now at

station, poised and waiting. The main feature of the elaborate operating room ritual—much of it as stylized as a high church service, as perfectly timed as ballet—was about to begin.

"Okay, Don," said Adam, "let's start the cutting."

In the Beechtree Inn—one of the more elegant country restaurants in the area—Kerri looked across the gleaming white linen tablecloth at Dave Tyler and was glad she had finally found the courage to call him. He was so grateful.

" . . . with all our close friends and relatives scattered to hellengone around the country," he was saying now, "and having been out of the social swim around here for quite awhile now because of Natalie's illness, I was really feeling very alone and getting much too slobbery with self-pity at the time you called. Frankly, I wasn't going to call you—I couldn't bring myself to impose this way on the generous nature of a virtual stranger."

"It's not an imposition, and besides, we're not strangers. I got to know and become very fond of Natalie, and she told me so many things about you."

"It's still a tremendous kindness on your part, and I'm very appreciative."

Kerri twiddled at the stem of her Manhattan glass (from which she'd taken only a few cautious sips) wishing she could think of something gay and witty to say to cheer him up, but the sense of Natalie's tragic end still hung over her like a heavy, invisible shroud.

"I'm only glad to be of any help I can in lessening your loneliness," she said.

"I know you mean that, but to tell the truth, I was a bit surprised when you called—I guess I thought you'd be offended or shocked by the unconventionality of Natalie's request." He looked at her with an apologetic little grin. "No offense meant, but you appear to me to be a fairly conventional type."

She smiled. "I'll have to agree with that, Mr. Tyler. I had a rural, churchy, very proper upbringing—and whether that's considered a virtue or a handicap these days, that's the way the twig was bent."

"We're a lot alike in that respect. I graduated from the Eagle Scouts into the gray flannel ranks. I always played by the rules. Natalie was just the opposite— completely unconventional. At first, I found it hard to take—" he lifted his scotch-on-rocks glass and gently joggled the ice cubes around on the bottom, his expression musing, "and then I discovered that beneath that flip, witty veneer of scorn she affected for so many of the socially proper things we're supposed to do, she had a core of absolute honesty and loyalty and—1-love—" His voice faltered, his eyes blurred and suddenly started streaming tears. He looked quickly down at the table, embarrassed and silent.

Good heavens, she thought in consternation, what does the nurses' manual say about the correct procedure with a crying, grownup man? After a few moments, she said brightly, "Shall we look over the menu and decide on dinner?"

"Please do, Kerri," he said gruffly, "but please excuse me if I don't join you just yet. Right now I couldn't face food. However, I would like another drink, if you don't object."

"Not at all. Whatever you want, Dave."

With the razor-sharp point of his scalpel, Adam lightly scratched a line across Holly's chest from armpit to armpit in a curving half-moon below the breasts down to the fourth pair of ribs. Quickly, he made a half-dozen short cuts across the line, which was fast turning crimson—the small marks would later guide the sur-

geons in matching the incision edges when sewing up the
wound after the operation.

"Look at the way her heart's leaping," remarked
Langsteen, the chief resident surgeon. The palpitations
were plainly visible. "Her head vibrates every time the
heart beats. Poor kid."

Adam was now going back over the line, cutting
deep. Wolff, on the other side of the table, now joined
in. Blood spurted as they cut deeper and deeper, working fast but with care, knowing that everything they
were cutting apart would have to be put back together
again. Soon they were peeling back the first layers of
tissue, and then each surgeon, aided by assistants,
worked at closing the severed vessels, some by electric
cautery and the larger ones with loops of suture quickly
knotted tight.

For about five minutes there were no sounds but the
sucking of suction pump, the rustling of gowns of the
instrument nurses as they swiftly passed instruments to
the surgeons, the short hisses of cauterizing, the muffled
whooshing of the mechanical lungs going on and off.
Adam straightened.

"The saw."

Ilse was already hovering behind him with the saw
readied. Taking it, Adam applied the blade to Holly's
chest. "All right, hit it."

Ilse switched on the current and the blade whirred
through breast bone. In a few moments he lifted it.

"That's it."

"So soon?" said Miss Vladek, the second instrument
nurse. "I didn't even hear you go through the ribs."

"They didn't pop in this one. Her bones are very
soft."

Again they went back to cutting, separating carti-
lages that held the ribs to the breastbone, teasing internal arteries into view for clamping before severing.
Langsteen and an intern worked with the retractors,

spreading the ribs, finally bringing into view the pericardium, the bag of tissue enclosing the heart. The
sound of it was strongly audible now, an irregular *thup,
thup thup*. The pulmonary artery was jerking violently
with each beat of the heart. Wolff put a finger against it
to feel the jets of high-pressure blood hammering
through. "Man! That's working harder than a sprinter
in a quarter-mile dash."

Adam had reached toward Ilse, who without a word
put scissors in his hands. Bending, he swiftly cut
through the pericardium. Wolff pulled back the loose
flaps of pericardial tissue, and at last it was in full view.

"Jesus," he said softly, "just look at that greedy
heart."

For a moment they all looked at the pulsating, enlarged mass of glistening purplish-pink organ. Wolff
looked across the table at Adam.

"Well, Adam—I guess now it's time to go to
work."

The BYOB (bring your own bottle) party at the Masse-
links was beginning to loosen up as the residents, interns, and nurses kept arriving in thickening numbers.
The hi-fi had been turned up, a few couples started
dancing, and Johnny Mathis, coming through strongly
on both the woofer and the tweeter, let out a deep male
groan as he launched into a soulful rendering of
"Chances Are".

Hal Lyons, dancing with Leila Frohm, said, "I didn't
know that guy was still around."

"He's back in style, and besides, I guess the Masse-
links are going in kind of heavy on the black music
tonight because, you know . . . the hospital staff is getting integrated."

"I see what you mean—" Hal was looking past her

shoulder—"and if the one coming in now is representative, I'm all for it."

With Donna Wheeler beside him, Steve Wolosyk moved with truculent aggressiveness into the apartment among the groups of guests. Under one arm he carried a brown paper bag of that peculiar wrinkling and shape that looked like nothing in the world other than what it was: a bottle of booze. Earlier, he had driven with Donna to a store in a nearby small town to pick up the bottle. Both had agreed on Scotch. She had insisted on paying for half of it, so he had insisted that she choose the brand.

"Let's try Black and White," she said without cracking a smile.

What had got Steve was the guarded awareness of them arising like an unpleasant odor from other customers in the store, most of them assuming utterly blank expressions that looked emptily through them or past them in a way he had suddenly found so intangibly insulting that he could barely refrain from doing something really crazy like going up to one of those hate-blanked faces and slapping the hell out of it.

In the car again driving to the party, Donna laughed. "Well, you asked for it." And then getting out the bottle, she'd expertly cut the seal with a fingernail and got off the cap and handed it to him. "Have a tranquilizer."

Steve savagely gulped down some of the raw stinging stuff and felt better. After all, this wasn't a big city where racial tolerance was taken for granted. This was the suburban apartheid belt in the Michigan belly where anti-black attitudes hadn't changed in decades, except to harden.

His anger, Steve knew, was really anger at himself, at old hotpants Wolosyk. His instant transition from nigger hater to nigger lover was a chemical miracle wrought by the color-blind gonads.

One of the guests, or perhaps it was the host, grinned

at the bottle under Steve's arm and said, "Glasses, ice, and mixes are in the kitchen."

The kitchen was mobbed, the air thick with cigarette smoke laden with booze and perfume. Everybody seemed to be talking at once:

"*. . . and all these microbes were milling around in this guy's belly, frantic as hell because they'd just got word the doctor was going to give him this new wonder antibiotic that was guaranteed to be 100% effective. 'Oh me oh my, oh me oh my!' they sobbed as they raced around, 'what are we going to do?' Until finally they noticed one old granddaddy of a microbe sitting off to one side grinning and smoking a big cigar, his little suitcase beside him. 'Why aren't you worried?' they asked him. 'Don't you realize that when this guy gets this new drug, we're all going to be dead?'*

"*Old granddaddy flicks off his cigar ash and says, 'Hell no, I'm not worried. I'm taking the eight o'clock shit out of here.'* "

Steve handed Donna her drink—Scotch with ice and, as she had specified, "plenty of water." He found the anonymity refreshing. The eyes that slid over them casually, couldn't have cared less.

"*. . . and after scraping out the gallstones and cutting a couple adhesions, I started looking around like the Old Man keeps telling us, you know, once you're in there anyway, you might as well give them a little bonus and take out the appendix too, so I scoop around in the guts, peeking under them and everywhere until I find this dinky little thing and excise it. Then along comes Joe and says, 'Jesus, man, that isn't the appendix!' I say 'Then what the hell is it?' and he says, 'I don't know, but it sure as hell isn't the appendix.' Meanwhile, the patient is getting ready to expire. 'What the Christ am I going to do now?' I ask Joe. 'Just close him up before Old Barr comes around and hope the hell that whatever it is, the guy won't miss it.'*

Now I challenge any of you—can you tell me what the hell the appendix looks like?"

Balancing their drinks, they maneuvered their way out of the kitchen.

"How do you like it so far?" Steve said.

"Frankly, I'm a little put out. This is the first white party I've been to where I'm not the center of attention."

seventeen

The buck always stops here, thought Adam as he looked down at the small body on the table. The *venae cavae* vein and left subclavian artery had already been severed, clamped and attached to the heart-lung machine. Everything else was in readiness. All the collected wisdom of fifty centuries of medicine had prepared the way for this moment—all of Holly's X-rays, the cath films, the sheets with the chemical equations, the recommendations of specialists, the calculated guesses, all the operation preliminaries—but the final responsibility for whether the patient lives or dies rests with the man who holds the knife, and on him alone.

"Pump on!" he said.

Chuck Jager, the heart-lung machine technician threw the switch, at the same time noting on his stop watch the exact time, which was 10:32, to be entered on his time records.

As the oxygenating pump whirred into action, sucking tired blood from Holly's body through the caval veins—to be renewed with pure oxygen before pumping back into her arteries—Adam bent anew over the table and inserted a dilating instrument through an incision already made by Wolff in the right ventricle. At the same time, Wolff and the resident pulled gently on threads that had been stitched into both sides of the four inch incision, thus opening the ventricle wide enough to afford a view inside the heart.

The defect was easy to see—an elongated hole larger than a silver dollar located high up in the membranous portion of the intraventricular septum.

"That's the worst I've ever seen," said Wolff. "The mystery to me is why she isn't dead."

"The high positioning cuts down on some of the blood backing up—but mostly it's just plain luck that she didn't fall off a fence, or try riding a bicycle, or some other crazy normal thing kids do, that's kept her alive." Adam was rapidly running his fingers along the roof of the ventricle, seeking the thin band of fibrous tissue he would need on which to anchor the patch— and not finding it. The tissues were stretched, deteriorated.

"Oh boy," Wolff said softly, "here's more bad news ... that other heart murmur I heard ..." With his scalpel he pointed to an almost hidden rupture on the lower side of an enlarged mitral orifice.

A chill slithered down Adam's spine. Most murmurs were not serious, but mitral insufficiency—in this case with a lesion resulting from stretching of the valvular ring under overloading pressures from left ventricular dilation—needed plastic repair.

"We'll have to fix it," he said.

"My God, Adam—we can't repair it! The extra twenty to thirty minutes it'd take—she'd never get off the table."

"If we don't get it now, she'd never last anyway—

and sure as hell could never survive another operation. This is the last and only chance."

Signaling with one hand, he called, "Dacron patch." His probing fingers had found the slight thickening of tissues that would have to serve as an anchoring rim for the patch—but dangerously near a heart valve.

First pinching the thin band between tissue forceps to form it into the anchoring perimeter, Adam took the Dacron and scissors from Ilse, and working with sculptural skill cut the patch to the size and shape necessary.

"Three-O silk."

Ilse had the medium-sized silk all readied in the atraumatic needles. Silk was the preferred suture material because it would last a lifetime.

Now began the grueling part. Each suture had a needle on each end. As Adam inserted one needle through the patch and tissue rim of the defect, Wolff grasped it with the needle-holding forceps and pulled it through. Each suture was to be tied separately one eighth inch apart, so that if one failed after the heart was closed, the whole patch would not loosen. It would take forty or fifty stitches, each a tedious, ticklish procedure in a most difficult location to get at.

The two surgeons worked with delicate speed, racing against time. They had about a dozen stitches in place when both noticed it at the same time—a sudden change in the heartbeat. The ventricles and auricles had started separate rhythms, no longer beating in unison.

"Adam," Wolff said soberly, "I think that last stitch hit a nerve."

"I'm afraid the heart's in block," Adam said just as soberly.

The chill of apprehension that telegraphed through the room could almost be felt. Heart block, or loss of synchrony, was an ominous sign. It could happen with the most meticulous surgeons because of the many invisible nerves passing through the interventricular wall into which Adam was sewing, with no way of knowing their precise location.

"Cut the needle and take out that last stitch," said Adam, "and let's hope——"

The sudden sound of the sliding doors from the induction room opening with an abrasive force never before known in OR-4 drew the startled eyes of everybody.

It was Victor Strang. Wearing a shantung summer suit and still carrying a dispatch case as if just arrived from the airport, he strode up to within a few feet of the operating table. His silvered hair was disheveled, his face stormy.

"Stop that operation!" he shouted. "It's unauthorized!"

Shocked faces watched. The blazing eyes had the look of insanity.

"You're irrational, Vic," said Adam, "and we're in the middle of a touch-and-go situation. Go somewhere and cool off and we'll discuss it afterwards."

"I said stop—I *order* it—STOP—!" Rushing up to the operating table, Strang began ripping aside the towel drapings. Everybody watched in horror. Plainly, the surgical chief had flipped. Also, having come into the operating room unscrubbed, he would be carrying most of the 60,000 bacterial micro-organisms normally found on any human skin.

"For God's sake, Vic," said Langsteen, catching Strang's arm and hauling him back a few feet. "You're contaminated!"

Even the circulating nurse—who like all others on the operating team had "scrubbed" with antiseptic soap for fifteen minutes before the operation—was considered "contaminated" simply because her duties required her to come and go from the operating room. All items she brought in were wrapped in sterile packs and she was never allowed to touch anything within. Even if she accidentally brushed against one of the scrubbed doctors or nurses, a sterile towel had to be pinned at once over the area she had touched.

"How *dare* you!" Face livid, eyes blazing, Strang struggled vigorously in the powerful grasp of Langsteen. "How dare—" The protestations and struggling abruptly ceased. Langsteen caught him under both arms as Strang stood unsteadily for a few moments, as if suddenly drunk.

"My God," said Wolff, looking at the odd pallor creeping over the director's stricken face, "he's having an infarct!"

"O-oxygen . . ." Strang gasped.

"Walter, get him into ICU," snapped Adam. "Jeff, you help. Do everything you possibly can, and we'll be in just as soon as we've finished here."

As the resident and the intern briskly helped Strang into the induction room, where there would be a wheeled stretcher, Adam turned toward the little body on the table.

"Come on, Don," he said with quiet fury, "now we've got to get that heart out of block and make up for lost time."

Hal Lyons, still dancing with Leila Frohm, said, "Am I that hard to take? Why do you keep twisting that lovely neck around to gawk at every clod who comes in?"

"I'm wondering why Chris is so late. He should have been here long ago."

"Waiting for him with baited breasts, huh?" He peered down at her ample mammary equipment, half bared in a low cut dress.

"Whenever you spout off those unfunny puns, I really worry about your medical future."

"My medical future is assured. Haven't you heard

that the AMA has taken over the mortgage on Fort Knox?"

"I wasn't worried about you—just the patients who'll have to listen to you."

"They'll die laughing."

"In stitches, too, I'll bet—at ten bucks a purl." A hand slid over her shoulder, and she turned.

"May I steal my girl back, please?" said Chris Holland.

Leila widened her eyes at him haughtily. "What's your excuse *this* time, Doctor?"

"I got held up. I had to implant a couple of vaginal pacemakers."

"Well, you'd better hope you have a strong battery," she said, and transferring herself to his arms, danced away.

Alone, Hal looked around for other interesting females and spotted Donna Wheeler dancing very slowly with Steve Wolosyk. He walked over, smiling broadly.

"Hey, haven't we met somewhere before?" he asked Donna.

"It depends on what circles you travel in."

"Only the very best. And I can tell you come from one of America's oldest families."

"Only second oldest. My ancestors missed the Mayflower and had to take reservations on the next boat over."

"Let's not be snobbish about it. Would you care to dance?"

She looked impishly up at Steve, who was glowering. "That's up to my date."

Hal grinned at Steve. "You must be one of the new interns, so I'm sure you won't mind if I exercise my preogative as a decrepit old resident and cut in on this dance?"

"My answer to that," said Steve, "is flake off, buster,

flake off." Grasping Donna more firmly around the waist, he swung back into the dance.

Returning from her rounds, Nurse Alice Burns heard the phone ringing at the fourth floor nurse's station and ran to get it.

"Miss Burns speaking."

"Alice—this is Kerri, and I have a problem."

Alice laughed knowingly. To her, a problem always involved a man, and Kerri Kozak—who shared an apartment with Alice—seemed strangely unknowledgeable about male nature. She'd known that Kerri had gone out on a date tonight, but not with whom.

"Uh, the gentleman I'm with isn't feeling well and can't drive, so—"

"You mean drunk?" Alice chortled. "So okay, you drive. What else?"

"The thing is, it could be terribly embarrassing if his neighbors saw him being driven home intoxicated by a strange woman."

"You mean he's married?"

"Uh, yes . . . but it isn't the way it sounds. I'll explain it all tomorrow."

"So what you're working up to is can you bring your gentleman back to the apartment and have me find another pad for the night. Right?"

"Well, yes . . . As a matter of fact, he's here right now. Asleep."

Alice laughed. "You astonish me, Kerri, but of course you can have the apartment tonight. I'll stay over at Peggy's."

"Thanks a load, Alice."

"Good night, Kerri. Enjoy yourself."

Shortly after midnight, Nurse Peggy Kraft, slightly tipsy, arrived at the fourth floor Nurses' station.

"Gosh, I'm sorry I'm late," she said to Alice Burns, whose shift had just ended.

"That's okay. Is there still any action at the party?"

"Not much, but if you hurry, you'll be in time to snag my date."

"I'm hurrying. Who is he?"

"Hal Lyons."

"Then there's no hurry. By the way, I've got a little favor to ask, Peg. Can I stay over at your place?"

"Sure, but why?"

"Kerri brought a guy back for the night."

"I don't believe it!"

"What's so surprising? She's a grownup girl now."

"Well, a couple guys I know think she's a little queer. They tell me she's stone cold dead from the neck down."

Alice's eyes flared. "If any guy ever said that to me about her, I'd slap him stone cold dead from the neck up!"

"Oh come on now, Alice. I know you're her roommate and closest friend and all that—and everybody knows *you're* straight—but doesn't Kerri ever, you know . . . hang around to peek at you in the shower, and stuff like that?"

"If she did," Alice snapped, "I wouldn't be blabbing it to a rattlemouth like you."

Peggy curtsied tipsily. "I beg your humble pardon. So I guess I guzzled too many."

"I'd really like to tell you a little secret, Peg, but I don't think I can trust you."

"I'm the soul of discretion when I'm sober and never remember a thing anybody tells me anyway when I'm crocked."

Alice looked dubious. "Well . . . I suppose it's better

if you knew the truth rather than go around spreading a lot of innuendos."

"What are they?"

"What some skunks slink around saying about people to hurt them."

"Now you listen here, Alice Burns—I've never said or done anything in my whole life to hurt a person!"

"Peg, what would you do if when you were still in high school, four of the 'nice' boys you knew sexually assaulted you?"

"Oh wowie!"

"I mean, if they put LSD or something like that in your coke and when you were half out of your mind, gangbanged you and left you on the ground outside of town until somebody came along and found you?"

"I'd grab the nearest machine gun," Peggy said hotly, "and shoot them all dead!"

"I only happen to know about this because once Kerri's brother came here on a visit and she got me to go on a date with him. He told me about it because he thought I could help her get over it. He said he and Kerri used to be very close, but ever since that thing happened, she became a little strange and aloof with him. Imagine—not even relaxed with her own brother."

"My God, an experience like that would be enough to turn any girl into a man-hater!"

"It's not hate, Peg. It's *fear*. She really likes men and she keeps trying, but she's just afraid of them."

"She's sure got problems."

"Just don't make them worse by any loose talk."

"I promise, Alice, cross my heart. And I'm sorry. I'd better go get some coffee before I grab a scalpel and stick it in the first guy that walks past."

"By the way, before you take a coffee break I think you'd better check Northrup in Recovery. When I did the rounds about twenty minutes ago, his BP was down."

"I'll do it right away so I can enjoy my coffee."

After checking Atlee Northrup—noting in particular that the urine bottle attached by catheter to his urethra was empty, a sure sign of a failing heart—Peggy sobered up considerably and scooted off to find the intern on duty.

The intern made his examination and at once called the "on call" resident.

"It's Northrup. His condition is deteriorating."

"What are the readings?"

"BP down to eighty-five, and dropping fast. Pulse one hundred. No urine output, temperature thirty-nine."

The resident gave a low whistle. "I'll be right over."

"Is there anything I can do until you get here?"

"Unless you've goofed on your readings, there's not a goddamn thing either of us can do. What's happened, he's bleeding around the graft in the chest cavity. Hemothorax. There's probably brain damage already."

"How about giving him blood and plasma?"

"Like pouring it down a hole. Nothing in the world could save him now except to cut him open in one helluva hurry and repair that fatal leakage. That's impossible for two reasons. Strang's in ICU with a whopping infarct—and Cane, Wolff and the whole damn operating bunch are tied up in OR-4. The second and best reason is the patient isn't recovered enough to go through all that again. He'd die on the table. I'm only coming over to doublecheck and keep my ass-guard up."

The intern hung up and said to Peggy, "You might as well save a little time and get out the death forms."

eighteen

Above the rhythmic chatter of the heart-lung machine, Adam called:

"Pump off!"

The technician threw the switch and sudden silence draped the room. Adam bent again over the patient to study his handiwork. The reconstruction of the heart and repair of the valve was finished. Now remained only the final check for errors—and a multitude of still-looming threats to Holly's existence, the most serious one being whether the frail body had enough reserve to survive the enormous damage that had been inflicted on it in this last-ditch battle to correct the fatal flaws.

The heart block, fortunately, had corrected itself within minutes, thanks to the speed with which Wolff had pulled out the misplaced suture. Had the heart not returned to normal rhythm, Adam would have resorted to the more drastic step of a pacemaking electrode—with a consequent loss of precious time. Since Holly had been in no immediate danger as long as she was still on the heart-lung machine, the two surgeons had raced on with the stitching.

Throughout the operation, Wolff had periodically released the aortic clamp just enough to let a little of the bright red oxygenated blood into the heart to nourish the heart muscles. After the suturing was finished, he released a full flow to check for leaks. Two small ones had been found and the stitches placed to close them.

"Keep your fingers crossed," Wolff said. "The heart action looks strong."

"I think we're ready to close her up, Don."

The long and complex job of closing the chest lasted until 1:56 A.M. As Wolff was putting in the final stitches, Adam signaled the anesthetist to shut off the gases.

Five minutes later, Holly opened her eyes and smiled, and then went back to sleep again.

"Stick with her for awhile, Don. I'm going over to see what can be done for Vic."

"Will do, Adam."

The long kiss ended.

"Is there any hope for me?" he said.

"There might be. At least you kiss well. With that kind of feeling, maybe you've got some soul, after all."

He bent toward her again. "One more try, and I promise I'll do better."

She slipped away. "That's enough for tonight. Let's not rush a good thing, Wolosyk."

nineteen

At 3:16 a.m., just nineteen hours and sixteen minutes after he had begun his career as an intern, Dr. Scott Walker was rudely shaken awake by the EW Admissions nurse.

"A call just came in," she said. "A girl beaten up."

"Oh God," he moaned. "I can't move. My body's rejecting me."

"The ambulance driver has all the details. He'll be around in a couple minutes to pick you up."

The fledgling doctor lumbered up out of the chair in which he had been snoozing. "Okay, okay . . . I'm off to a running start."

Shortly after 4:00 A.M., Mike Tunstra was driving through misty drizzle up the hospital entrance road when the EW ambulance streaked past him with a brief whine of a siren. More meat for us, he thought with a sour grin. They'd sure been piling up down in Path lately.

Not that he minded too much. In another two or three weeks, he'd be able to quietly resign and become a rich fat cat for about the next ninety-nine years before it was his turn to get dumped on a cold slab by some jerk orderly.

After parking, he noticed they were just unloading the meat wagon at the EW entrance and having trouble with the patient, so just out of curiosity he ambled over.

The girl on the stretcher was black and almost naked except for a few remnants of ripped clothing, and her face was a mutilated, bloodied mess. She battled against the restraining hands of the intern, screaming hysterically.

" . . . *stop, stop—keep yo' motherfuggin' hands off me! I already tell yo' everything I know about Speed an' yo' fuggin' H! Now yo' stop—!"*

Mike felt a slither of apprehension. That wild tumbleweed of hair, the shrill voice, skinny figure . . . The same chick who'd brought Speed to the hospital.

"That broad's really had it," he said to the intern. "Do you think she'll pull through?"

"She'll live," said the intern, "but she'll never be pretty again."

Chilled, Mike hurried away through the drizzling, pre-dawn murk. Now the cops could get her testimony about the suitcase.

Far worse, she'd already squealed to the Mafia goons who'd creamed her.

Double-timing it to the rear entrance to the basement, he let himself in with his employee's key and trotted on down to the morgue. After midnight the morgue was unattended until the morning shift came in at 8:00 A.M., which gave him plenty of time, but he was anxious to get it over with.

First taking the precaution of locking the morgue door behind him—there was always the chance that somebody would die during the night and be brought down—he hustled on to the staff locker area. There he opened his own locker and got out all the necessary tools, which were stashed away in a brown paper bag, and the heavy black suitcase. Carrying these, he made his way into the macabre, clammy precinct of the dead and turned on the lights above the row of cold storage lockers.

Selecting the one that contained the cadaver of Speed Wilson, he slid open the long locker drawer, pulled off the sheet, and went to work.

It was the most gruesome ten minutes of Mike's life, and each second oozed past like a slow-motion nightmare in a charnel house. The first problem was straightening the arms away from the chest because now they had fully stiffened with rigor mortis. Heaving and twisting at the bent arms, for a moment he had the ghastly illusion that the corpse had come to life and was fighting back with muscles of iron. In the frenzy of battle, the corpse slid off the table, clumping like a side of beef against the floor and giving out squashy sounds of loose stuff heaving around inside. It took all the frantic efforts he could muster to get it back on the table again.

Another thing that got him was that somebody had done a bad job of closing the mouth, so the corpse kept grinning at him like the eighty-eight pearly white keys of a Steinway all through the queasy, slobbery job of hauling out his guts. He hadn't foreseen that. The path chief had kept only tissue samples and put most of the organs back. In unanticipated need of a receptacle, Mike dumped the bloody mess into the empty black suitcase. When there wasn't quite enough room to stuff all the plastic bags of heroin into the shell of chest and belly, he fished around inside and managed to find a few more handfuls of slippery, smelly glop to pull out. Then he sewed up the cadaver again, using the baseball overhand stitch used by the pathologists.

By that time, his stomach was churning and he was so nauseated he was afraid he would vomit but held himself in tight because he still had to get the corpse stowed back in the storage locker, clean up, then get rid of the suitcase.

What a helluva crappy tough way to become a millionaire, he thought in disgust.

Lugging the leaking suitcase down the corridor toward the incinerator, where he intended to dispose of the bag and its load of human entrails, he began to feel better. The first big hurdle was behind, the lifetime supply of bread a lot closer.

A few seconds later he had a small setback. The incinerator was already in use. One of the night custodians was lazily removing waste from a big canvas disposal cart and shoving it into the incinerator opening, plainly in no hurry.

Annoyed, Mike backed away afraid he might have been seen. He darted down another corridor leading toward the exit—he couldn't put it in his locker—he could smell the contents. He'd have to dump it in one of the big metal garbage cans outside.

When he got outside it was still drizzling, still dark and murky. He started toward the garbage disposal area and had gone only a few steps when something hard poked against his ribs.

"Okay—put it down."

With a clutching, sinking sensation of dismay, he started turning and the hard snout of a gun jabbed against him again.

"The suitcase, punk—put it down!"

Carefully he put the suitcase down. "Now look, I don't know a thing about this suitcase—" he started babbling at the two men who stood there, both wearing pale rainhats and raincoats, both holding guns— "I just found it in the locker room and was going to report it to—"

"Just get the hell out of here," snapped one of the men, "and forget you ever saw it."

The sick shock lifted, soared into jubilance as the two men strode away, one lugging the suitcase. My God, they weren't cops after all. He'd pulled it off!

But the next moment, the horrifying truth hit him. If not cops, they had to be Mafia.

What would they do to him when they found out what was really in the suitcase?

twenty

Awakening, Kerri lay luxuriating for awhile in a dreamy, half-sleep state of utter happiness, slowly emerging into full wakefulness. Afar in the gray murk of dawn she heard the wail of a train whistle, the stolid drone of trucks on the freeway, the searing, stabbing sound of a jet plane passing overhead. Familiar, dull everyday sounds, yet somehow rich and vivid, throbbing with a new sense of life all around her.

Turning, she saw that he was still sunk in sleep, one arm still around her. She lay back again, looking at the ceiling. She did not want to break his perfect sleep, which she knew he had gotten from her.

From yesterday's viewpoint, the happenings of last night would have shocked her. Now it all seemed so simple, natural, and right.

The hysteria of weeping that had seized him was not from overdrinking, but from unassuageable grief. She had turned over the bedroom to him, making her own bed on the living room couch, and later, hearing the sounds that were so much like those of a lost child in need of help, she had gone to him in the darkness of the bedroom, thinking to offer comforting words. His reaching out for her—the sense of his being shorn suddenly from the abundance of Natalie's love and groping blindly in his bereavement for human warmth and closeness—had filled her with an overwhelming tenderness for him. She quickly lay down alongside him and pulled his head close to the hollow of her neck and shoulder. He was quivering uncontrollably. "Never mind," she whispered shakily as her own tears ran into her mouth. "Everything heals . . ." He buried his head between her breasts, like a child clinging intensely to her, and with trembling hands she held him tight. Even then she had a prescience of boundaries, defenses, melting away, but some of the terrible fractional violence of death had filled her, as it did him, and she had no power at this crisis to turn him away.

Then his arms were strong and warm around her, clinging to her in a surge of gratitude, and she knew without really thinking about it that she would yield to him whatever she could. Her arms clasped around his hard back and she could sense the pain was easing from his heart, that she was helping to banish the dreadful pictures from his mind as the pent-up darkness of death was slowly leaving his body under the pulsing inflow of new life. And soon, for the first time in her life, her passion was ignited. Quite suddenly, in the depths of her body, a wondrous feeling glowed into life from where before there had been nothingness. She was unaware of her own short wild cries as the rapture built to a crescendo.

It had been beautiful, marvelous, a miracle.

Later, while he slept, she lay motionless, eyes staring into darkness. He had been so like a wounded creature, now soothed and restored and softly healing. She could not sleep for the wonder of it. Some of the new life that had made him whole again had also wrought changes in her. Her consciousness was flooded with it—alive with replays of her childhood, her girlhood, and all the forgotten incidents and the dark influences she had forced from memory. No longer did any of it frighten her. It was as if she understood all the evil, all the good, and was able to draw from the darkness of the past a new strength. She, too, in her own way had been restored.

If there was any new wisdom she had learned, it was in the joy of giving, no longer to be in fear of the taking.

Carefully extricating herself from his sleeping embrace, she got out of bed and quietly went about her usual morning preparations. When he awoke, she would be gone, probably never to see him again. But it would not be just a ships-passing-in-the-night sort of thing. Her warmth would remain with him, and his with her.

Rosemary Clugg began the first of her top priority chores for the day by putting through a call to Mrs. Atlee Northrup in exclusive Bloomington Heights.

Awakened by her reluctant maid a full hour before her usual time for getting up, Christina Northrup got on her bedroom phone a few minutes later with a peevishness in her voice that impelled Rosemary to come bluntly to the point:

"This is the supervisor of nurses at Tri-County hospital, Mrs. Northrup. It is my sad duty to inform you that your husband was unable to survive surgery and passed away during the night."

"But Dr. Strang himself promised me that he would personally keep me advised!"

"Dr. Strang would have called you, but unfortunately he is unavailable, due to a sudden illness."

"Oh dear, I'm so sorry to hear that. I do hope it's nothing serious."

The supervisor of nurses wasn't sure she'd heard correctly. "I'm afraid you misunderstand, Mrs. Northrup. Your husband is dead."

"But you're so wrong—Atlee has only been *released*. Poor Atlee could never overcome the enslavement of his senses, you know, but now that he's freed of his prison of flesh, his soul, his beautiful spirit can soar. It is nothing tragic at all, only the beginning of a marvelous new existence, and dear Atlee will be so much happier now."

Convinced that she was talking to a nut, Rosemary continued with the rest of the details. "One of the routine questions I must ask you, Mrs. Northrup, is will you authorize us to perform an autopsy on your late husband?"

"No, no, no—it could disturb psychic rhythms and heavens only knows what else!"

"And you will make arrangements with a mortuary?"

"Yes indeed. Have Atlee ready, and a vehicle shall be there this forenoon to remove his remains."

twenty-one

Adam looked up from the X-rays, the cardiograms, the test results.

"What's your opinion, Don?" he asked Wolff.

The chief resident's face was grim. "As you can see, even the anterior wall of the heart is involved. The anesthetist tells me he can maintain the blood pressure only with pressor drugs given intravenously. The nurse reports almost no urine output. Twice they had to put him on electric pacing. I'd say all signs point to Vic's death within two or three days from shock and heart failure."

"How much of this does Vic know as yet?"

"After all, Adam, Vic's the guy who could write the book. When he regained consciousness, still only half there, his brain was already grappling with self-diagnosis—and surprisingly accurate. He knows he's facing the curtain."

"Don't you think it would be a mistake for me to risk upsetting him with a visit?"

"It would upset him more if you don't. He insists on seeing you."

Following the operation on Holly last night, Adam had gone to ICU where Victor Strang was still unconscious and under oxygen, being tended by Langsteen and another cardiac resident. Later, Wolff joined them and it was decided that the residents would remain on constant, all-night duty with the patient, meanwhile taking all tests possible. Adam and Wolff, deeply exhausted from the long hours of surgery, would stay in quarters at the hospital and get all the sleep they could, subject to immediate call in the event the patient regained consciousness or took a sudden turn for the worse.

Now—ten hours after being struck down by his coronary disease—Strang had been out of his coma for about a half hour.

"All right, Don," said Adam, "I'll go see what Vic has to say."

In the corridor he encountered Glenna Woods, who hastily averted her eyes. Anger rose up in Adam.

"You're the one who called Dr. Strang last night, aren't you?" he said tightly. "I hope you realize if hadn't been for that—"

Glenna bowed her head, both hands covering her face, and fled.

Adam's anger melted. In attempting to hurt him by tattling to Vic, she had become her own victim.

In ICU, Victor Strang lay amid a conglomeration of tubes and monitoring wires sprouting from various parts of his body. His face was pallid, only a ghost of his former self.

"I guess we don't have to mince any words, do we, Adam?" The surgical director's voice was weak and hollow. "You've seen the tests. It's pretty bad, isn't it?"

"Do you want to hear my opinion as a patient or a surgeon?"

"I'm still a surgeon, Adam."

"Then I'll have to say it's hopeless."

Strang managed a ghastly grin. "*Touche*. You've got a touch of the bastard in you, Adam—enough to be a great surgeon."

"I'm only giving my medical opinion as honestly as I can. A quarter of your heart is ischemic, and it's creeping. There's no possible way by artificial means that we can increase the blood supply to prevent continuing tissue damage. My prognosis is twenty-four hours. With luck."

"But there is a way! A by-pass would stop the ischemia."

"Not only would it have to be a double by-pass— that's a dangerously long time on the pump—but there's the additional problem of ostial stenosis."

"But with the right surgeon?"

"That brings us up to the worst problem—time. I'm sure there are a few top heart surgeons in the country who could and would drop all other commitments to fly in to attempt such an operation for you—if they could get here in time. But we can give it a try. Give me a few names of surgeons of your choice, in priority, and we'll contact them immediately."

The pale blue eyes gleamed. "I'm asking you, Adam! You're the first priority surgeon of my choice."

Adam was astonished. "That's quite a flip-flop in your attitude."

"Adam, I'm going to eat humble pie. Among the many mistakes I've made, the biggest one I'm guilty of was in bearing down so hard on you. Part of it resulted from my own conceit and self-deception, but now I'm facing the ultimate truth that none of us can ever escape—death. There's no time left for lies or personality analysis. I don't know of any surgeon more qualified than you are; including myself."

"But—under the circumstances—are you sure you have that much faith in me?"

"What better proof of my faith than my readiness to put my life in your hands in an operation that might well turn out to be the most precarious, difficult one of your career? Now hop to it and see how fast you can get the ball rolling."

"It's rolling, Vic—" Adam started out—"we'll have you on the table in a few hours."

In the wide open doorway at the loading ramp behind the morgue, Orderly Mike Tunstra nervously watched the county welfare department panel truck back into place. The driver, a short, stocky, middleaged guy in green denim workclothes, and a kid of about nineteen, similarly dressed, hopped out. The older one held a sheaf of thin green, white, yellow and blue shipping papers, with carbons, which he now checked.

"We're here, authority of the police department," he said importantly, "to pick up a deceased by name of William Wilson."

"He's all ready and waiting," said Mike, "get the back of your truck open and I'll get him."

Hustling back to the lockers just outside the morgue in the loading area—put there especially to facilitate the departure of the morgue guests—he rolled out one of the drawers and managed with a little clumsy maneuvering to get the cadaver shifted over on a wheeled stretcher. Normally, the *diener*, Clem Jackson would have been there to help, but earlier he had insisted to Clem that he could handle the loading alone for a couple hours and urged him to take a long coffee break to make up for Mike's failure to help Clem with the dirty work at the autopsy yesterday.

Mike's nervousness increased when the two from the welfare department helped him roll the stretcher into the back of the panel truck.

"Don't you have your own stretcher to move him onto?" he said.

"Naw, we'll just dump him into this box we brought along. He might as well get used to it because he's gonna live in it for a long time."

When they pulled the sheet off, Mike's heart was jumping like mad for fear they'd be suspicious. The tag tied to the big toe of the cadaver said *William Wilson,* but the body was white and that of Atlee Northrup.

The idea—the solution Mike had been diligently seeking—had come to him in a flash right after he found out that the latest arrival in the morgue was not to be autopsied and was scheduled to be picked up by a mortuary that very morning. By simply switching the identification tags, Atlee Northrup would be trucked off to be buried in a pauper's graveyard reserved for criminals and the indigent, and William (Speed) Wilson would be whisked off by limousine to a fancy funeral parlour.

The switch, of course, would be quickly discovered by the mortician, but the pay-off of Mike's latest brainstorm was to go chasing after the hearse in about fifteen minutes in an EW meat wagon (to which he had a key) and explain that a terrible mix-up of identities had occurred and he'd come to take back the body that had been picked up by mistake.

And somewhere along the way on the trip back, he'd park and get the heroin out of Speed's corpse and find a place to stash it. Just where he hadn't yet decided.

"Crissake, for a guy headed for potter's field," said the driver, "he sure looks well fed. It's gonna be a tight fit, squeezin' him into this box."

Mike was sweating a little when he rolled the empty stretcher back into the loading area.

One more hurdle behind. Bigger ones still ahead.

About a half hour later, a phantom gray hearse arrived. On its side, printed in elegant small letters, was, *Chapel Of The Eternal Spirit,* and beneath that, *Complete, Efficient, Dignified Service.*

Mike hurried to get the body of Speed Wilson loaded onto a stretcher, and was just rolling it toward the ramp when a familiar voice jarred the hell out of him.

"Hey you, Tunstra—I've got things to say to you . . ."

He turned and saw Sergeant Borman approaching.

twenty-two

"Adam—"

He turned, at first not recognizing the attractive blonde woman. Then, "Mrs. Strang—we tried to call you last night, but—"

"I know. I was out for the evening and only got the message this morning. And now they won't let me in to talk to Vic. How is he?"

"His condition is critical." Briefly, Adam told her the facts.

Leslie Strang nibbled at her lovely lips, frowning. "I've been very rotten toward Vic lately, and I feel terribly responsible."

"But this isn't any overnight development, Mrs. Strang, and—"

"Please, Adam—not so much formality. Call me Leslie before I start feeling my age."

Adam smiled. "All right, Leslie—what I was about to say, Vic's heart disorder obviously has a long-standing history, and there's nothing for you to feel responsible about."

"But there is. A couple nights ago—following a pretty nasty quarrel—I finally dug it out of Vic, about the angina he's been concealing for so long, and it's made me feel quite differently about him. He's been rather heroic, I think—although stupidly so—in carrying on his job all these years without any complaints or apologies or martyring himself to me. Had I known the truth, well . . . I would have changed my lifestyle . . ."

"Had he kept us all informed, we might have helped him before it got this far."

"I know. Vic just can't bear to reveal things about himself. Has he told you about the syringomyelia?"

"Don't tell me he thinks he's got that!"

"But definitely. Apparently that's what's been gnawing at him so much recently. He told me about the symptoms starting in his hands that could ruin him as a surgeon."

Adam was astonished. "But he can't be sure it's syringomyelia—not without exhaustive tests. There are other ailments with similar symptoms. Neurogenic arthropathy, for example—that can be diagnosed by x-ray. It could be a neurologic lesion, or possibly a spinal cord tumor. These things are operable and curable, and even if it's syringomyelia, there's new research being done that's very promising . . ."

"You'll do all you can to make him well again, won't you, Adam?"

"Everything humanly possible."

"Before the operation, may I say a few words to him? I want him to know that . . . things are going to be different."

"Of course. We want everything going for him that we can get."

"Thank you, Adam, dear . . ." She leaned close and

kissed him on the cheek and he felt the trickle of a tear she left there.

By mid-morning, Holly Robbins was transferred from the recovery room back to the Children's Pavilion. Nearly nine hours had passed since she left the operation with a reconstructed heart. Although still connected to various monitoring wires and her existence still partially dependent on technology, her blood pressure was up to 82/60, a good sign, and her face had a pinkish color that hadn't been there in years.

After she was installed and a nurse came around to check—a nurse she'd never seen before—Holly made another try. "Would you play a game of S.O.B. with me?"

"Sure," said the nurse. "I'll get the cards . . ."

twenty-three

Exultant, Mike jammed the gas pedal all the way down. In the hospital meat wagon he could break all speed limits and the cops wouldn't bother him, and if he wanted to, just for the hell of it, he could use the siren to clear traffic ahead.

He felt on a high from the speed, the wind slamming through the vents—and from knowing the end was in sight.

That pig, Sergeant Borman had held him up, but the breaks were still coming his way. As it turned out, Borman's bark had been a lot worse than his bite.

"Let's have another little talk about that suitcase, Tunstra," the sergeant had said.

"Excuse me," said Mike hurriedly, because by then the gray hearse had parked and its driver was getting out, "I've got to tell this guy where to find the meat."

And to the driver, "You're here to pick up Northrup?"

"Righto."

"He's in that second locker—you'll see the name on the tag. You need any help?"

"Nope. I got a helper with me."

Sweating, but also grinning a little, because Mike had learned from many past situations that the tighter the spot you're in, the more you had to brazen it out, he said, "Just handle him gently—he's the sensitive type." Then had hustled out of the loading area, forcing Borman to follow if he wanted to talk.

"Okay," he told the cop, "so what's all this crap about a suitcase?"

For nearly an hour, Borman had put him through a lot of stupid but also artful questioning doubtless intended to trip him up, but Mike's animal cunning didn't let him down. He guessed that the cops had caught the guys with the suitcase full of human entrails but beyond that had only suspicions.

With growing certainty that they had nothing on him, he said finally, impatiently, "Can we break it off now, sergeant? It's been delightful, but I've got work to do."

"Why are you sweating, Tunstra? Too much mental strain?"

Mike held his snotty grin. "It's the ghosts I keep seeing. This place is fulla them."

"Well, damn soon now you're going to be haunted by a couple more real bad ones." The sergeant shoved his interrogation pad back in a hip pocket. "The two shit-heelers I'm referring to were spotted early this morning sneaking across the fence behind the hospital lugging a suitcase. They got picked up by a car, and as soon as they found out they were being tailed, tried for a getaway. They didn't have good tires for wet roads at a hundred per and slammed against a concrete abutment and rolled on over into an underpass about forty feet below. There's nothing much left of them—just guts splattered all over the place."

"Are you trying to accuse me of that, too, Sergeant?"

"It's just perfunctory, Tunstra, just perfunctory interrogation we gotta go through. So now I'll leave you alone with the ghosts for awhile."

The Chapel of the Eternal Spirit was set back on a couple acres of rich green lawn fenced in by a low stone wall and landscaped with heavy rows of shrubbery and bright burst of flowers.

Mike parked the ambulance in the mortuary parking area, surprised to find that it was almost filled up with expensive big cars. He could hear the sad strains of churchy organ music drifting from the chapel itself, which was a low structure of stone with stained glass windows and a big concrete cross towering above the entrance.

Just inside the door, he was stopped by a snobbish looking guy wearing an afternoon cutaway jacket, ascot, and striped gray-and-white trousers. He frowned at Mike's hospital garb.

"You can't come in now," he said in a mellifluous whisper. "The service has just started."

"Service for who?"

"The late Atlee Northrup."

"But they can't . . . I mean, I've got to see the body . . ."

The elegant jacket nodded in the direction of a minister who had just begun to speak in a funereal tone even more mellifluous than the usher's.

"Brethren, we are gathered here . . ."

"Where's the casket?" said Mike.

The usher raised his eyebrows. "There's no casket . . ." He leaned toward Mike, turning his head in the direction of the speaker. "See that urn in front of the minister? All that's left of Mr. Northrup is in that little jar . . ."

Mike stared, horrified. "You mean this is a *crematorium?*"

"But of course. It's the most dignified, efficient way, don't you think? And it's so much more consoling to those who remain." The usher allowed himself a sneaky smile. "As a matter of fact, Mrs. Northrup plans to have her own columbarium built into her living room for the urn, so that every day she can sit there and commune with her husband's spirit."

At 4:15 P.M., Ilse Jensen, first instrument nurse, looked up only long enough to smile briefly at Adam Cane as he entered the operating room and was helped by the second instrument nurse into his gown and gloves. He glanced across the draped body on the table at Don Wolff, already gloved and gowned.

"Okay, Don," said Adam, "let's prove to Vic that we've learned a thing or two."

*free catalog of hundreds of your △ books

Now it's easy to get the paperbacks you want to read! Choose from hundreds of popular-priced books in your favorite categories and order them conveniently, by mail!

write to PYRAMID BOOKS

MAIL ORDER DEPARTMENT
9 Garden Street
Moonachie, New Jersey 07074

M01

Magnificent, illustrated excursions far beyond the reaches of the known . . .

Please send me: _____DEVILS & DEMONS, A Dictionary of Demonology, J. Tondriau & R. Villeneuve. A complete guide to all demonology, fully describes every known demon; details the rites and terms of the satanic arts; traces the times, places and bloody history of satanism while shedding light on its dark workings. Ill. with b & w and color drawings. Y2718 — $1.95

_____THE OCCULT, Secrets of the Hidden World, J. Tondriau. Legendary sorcerers . . . orgies of a Witches' Sabbath . . . rites of the Knights Templars . . . disciplines of Yoga . . . investigations of precognition in modern universities . . . uses of the Tarot . . . and much more in a single volume of occult knowledge. Ill. with b & w and color drawings, charts. H2719 — $1.65

_____HISTORY OF ASTROLOGY, Science or Superstition?, S. Hutin. The geological and chronological expanse of astrology, from man's first recorded history to the present. Ill. with b & w and color photos and drawings, charts. H2716 — $1.65

_____THE WORLD OF MAGIC, Practitioners of the Unexplained, E. de Martino. The complete history of magic: the other reality that even logical men cannot deny. Reveals great "tricks" and the secrets of their masters, and many fascinating, unexplainable magical feats. Ill. with b & w drawings and rare photos. D2720 — $1.45

_____ZEN: The Art of Life, R. Linssen. Zen Buddhism is the most concrete, yet most elusive of disciplines. This book presents the complete history of Zen and other major movements. Also, a unique study of the affects of Zen on painting, poetry, intellectual endeavor, and everyday life. Ill. with b & w and color drawings and photos. D2717 — $1.45

Send to:
PYRAMID PUBLICATIONS, Dept. M.O., 9 Garden Street, Moonachie, N. J. 07074

NAME _____
ADDRESS _____
CITY _____
STATE _____ ZIP _____

I enclose $_____ , which includes the total price of all books ordered plus 25¢ per book postage and handling if the total is less than $5.00. If my total order is $5.00 or more, I understand that Pyramid will pay all postage and handling. Please allow three to four weeks for delivery.

3

ON SALE NOW WHEREVER PAPERBACKS ARE SOLD —
or use this handy coupon to order directly from the publisher.

**The Pyramid
Healthful Living Series**

HEALTH & NUTRITION

paperbacks for
**EVERYTHING
YOU WANT
TO KNOW
ABOUT . . .**

This is the most complete, continuing series of basic books on health foods, nutrition and natural lifestyles available from a single U.S. publisher. These days, "you are what you read," and Pyramid's ABOUT books might help you be the person you want to be.

Please send me:

_____HONEY BT2662 — 75¢
_____YOGURT BT2663 — 75¢
_____YEAST BT2664 — 75¢
_____WHEAT GERM
       BT2665 — 75¢
_____VITAMINS BT2666 — 75¢
_____MOLASSES BT2667 — 75¢
_____SLIMMING BT2668 — 75¢
_____SEA FOODS
       BT2669 — 75¢
_____SOYA BEANS
       BT2670 — 75¢
_____GARLIC BT2671 — 75¢
_____FASTING BT2672 — 75¢
_____ALLERGY BT2673 — 75¢
_____LOW FAT DIET
       BT2804 — 75¢
_____HOME MADE WINES
       BT2805 — 75¢
_____SALT-FREE RECIPES
       BT2806 — 75¢
_____EATING FOR HEALTH
       BT2807 — 75¢
_____CONSTIPATION
       BT2808 — 75¢
_____ASTHMA & BRONCHITIS
       BT2809 — 75¢

Send to:
PYRAMID PUBLICATIONS,
Dept. M.O., 9 Garden Street,
Moonachie, N. J. 07074

NAME_____
ADDRESS_____
CITY_____
STATE_____ ZIP_____

I enclose $_____ , which includes the total price of all books ordered plus 25¢ per book postage and handling if the total is less than $5.00.
If my total order is $5.00 or more, I understand that Pyramid will pay all postage and handling.

No COD's or stamps. Please allow three to four weeks for delivery.

2

MIRACLE, MAKE-BELIEVE OR MATTER-OF-FACT?

You will not read a more important new book this year!

Just published . . . this is the book that can totally satisfy your interest and curiosity in *acupuncture,* the ancient Chinese practice of needle medicine, currently a subject of great controversy. Acupuncture is based on thousands of years of complex theories and history, but the book **ACUPUNCTURE** by Marc Duke makes it both understandable and exciting.

• Fully ill. with ancient and new charts and diagrams • Dramatic photos recently taken in China, never before published • Authentic source material researched and translated by the author from the original Chinese • A selection of the Book Find Club and the Book-of-the-Month Club.

If you wonder why Americans are being denied the real benefits—the "miracles"—of *acupuncture* that many other nations of people enjoy, then you must read this book.

Please send me_____copies of ACUPUNCTURE (hardcover) 9303—$6.95

I enclose $_____

Send to:
PYRAMID PUBLICATIONS, Dept. M.O., 9 Garden Street, Moonachie, N. J. 07074

NAME_____

ADDRESS_____

CITY_____

STATE_____ZIP_____

No COD's or stamps. Please allow three to four weeks for delivery.